Praise for the works of Bette Hawkins

In My Heart

Set in 1958 in small-town Southern US and focused on the early days of the country music circuit, this is a really sweet and gentle romance. The setting gives it a bit of a nostalgic feel, but Hawkins keeps things realistic and the setting comes alive. Hawkins provides enough detail to set the scene and give the reader a feeling of being in the moment without resorting to dumping information and context. Narrated by Alice, *In My Heart* follows her struggle to find her place in the world. There's a wonderful innocence and inner strength in Alice— smothered by her life in a small southern US town, she wants more than to follow in the footsteps of her mother and sister, she wants to make her own way in the world and make her own mark. I especially appreciated that Hawkins wrote Alice within the context of the time and place—in some novels, the main characters openly, and rather unrealistically, challenge the societal norms but Alice's resolution and rebellions are subtle and small…This isn't a long book but Hawkins uses the time she has with the reader to focus on the characters and creates a wonderfully sweet romance.

- C-Spot Reviews

In My Heart is a well-written romance with good pacing and dialogue. The interesting plot is about two strong talented women, country music, small-town mindset, being different… All in all, a really enjoyable story which I will read again. I recommend it, and am looking forward to the next book by the author.

- Pin's Reviews - goodreads

Like a Book

Like a Book is Bette Hawkins's second book and it has a lot of good things going for it (especially June!). If you enjoy contemporary romances, especially those set in Australia, you should check this one out. I look forward to seeing what's next from this author.

- The Lesbian Review

No More Pretending

I don't know what it is, but something about romances that involve a movie star falling in love with a girl-next-door type, are some of my favorites. I must be honest, this book was not on my radar at all. Therefore, it was such a pleasant surprise how much I really enjoyed this. Then to find out this is a debut novel, I'm even more impressed. The way she writes is believable and I thought contained good dialogue. For me, she successfully "showed" the romantic connection, and that's what I look for in a romance author.

- Lex Kent's Reviews - *Goodreads*

Running Deep

Other Bella Books by Bette Hawkins

In My Heart
Like a Book
No More Pretending

About the Author

Bette lives in Melbourne with her girlfriend and dogs. She loves travel, music, cinema, playing the guitar, and cooking. She's passionate about lesbian stories.

Running Deep

Bette Hawkins

BELLA
BOOKS
2020

Bella Books, Inc.
P.O. Box 10543
Tallahassee, FL 32302

Printed in the United States of America on acid-free paper.

First Bella Books Edition 2020

Editor: Ann Roberts
Cover Designer: Judith Fellows

ISBN: 978-1-64247-117-5

Acknowledgment

Thanks to my sweet Hazel, and everyone at Bella Books.

CHAPTER ONE

2000 Olympic Trials - Sydney

The announcer introduced Hannah, and the spectators cheered. As she stepped up to the block she reminded herself to smile, waving to the crowd.

She adjusted her goggles and stared into the pool while the announcer moved on to her competitors. She focused on the shimmering water that lay beneath her feet. Her underwhelming qualifying time had placed her in the first lane. Having an empty one beside her would cut down on distractions, and she didn't mind that her lane meant nobody thought she was going to win.

For the past eighteen months, a mantra had looped through Hannah's mind. It played in time with every stroke. At five in the morning, when she dragged herself out of bed to train, her feet hit the floor to the rhythm of the words.

She was going to win this race. She *had* to win this race.

Hannah gazed into the water so she wouldn't have to look at the spectators, but she was attuned to each sound they made. There were thousands of people shouting, stamping their feet, and clapping. They weren't just watching for her, but there was feverish speculation about her prospects from every newspaper and trashy magazine in the country. Coming out of retirement had been a secret for as long as she could get away with it. By now, photographers were following her around, circling like vultures to stick their cameras in her face. The press had grown even more intrusive since she'd last competed.

Hannah sensed the media was poised to tip the narrative one way or the other, comeback stories half-written and waiting for this next chapter. If she qualified for the hometown Olympics, she would be a phoenix rising from the ashes. If she failed, she would be their cautionary tale, a fallen hero who'd overreached. Too old, and who did she think she was, trying to snatch a spot on the team away from more deserving contenders?

Even if she could block out the ascending rows upon rows of the audience, there was one person whose presence she could never ignore, no matter how hard she wanted to try.

Angie Thompson stood at the pool's side, watching her. Weeks ago, Hannah caught a segment on *Sports Weekly* about Angie joining the Australian coaching team. After that story, Hannah endured sleepless nights contemplating pulling out, just so she wouldn't have to deal with Angie.

For years, Hannah was confident they would never see one another again. An ocean separated them, along with so much time. That part of her life was squared away in a box on the highest shelf, and she wouldn't allow herself to dwell on it.

Their eyes met before Hannah shifted her gaze back to the water. There were a lot of things about Angie that were just as Hannah remembered. In the footage on the morning show, Hannah noticed Angie's warm green eyes and the way they creased at the corners when she smiled.

There were many differences too. They'd been only kids the last time they'd seen one another in person. Angie's honey-brown hair fell in waves, longer and thicker now that she didn't have to deal with chlorine damage. The warm blond highlights suited her. Since retiring from swimming, she had put on weight that she wore well. She was all soft curves these days.

After watching the segment, Hannah looked into her own brown eyes in the mirror to check for lines. She didn't think she'd changed that much, but how could she know for sure? Her black hair was still cut just above her shoulders, and her skin had cleared since then. After some time away from the industry, she'd gotten back into shape.

If she qualified today, she couldn't avoid Angie. The best she could hope for was that any awkwardness passed quickly, but she might be making too much of it. Angie loomed large in her history, but there was no way of knowing if the reverse was true.

The crowd was quiet now, holding a collective breath as they waited for the race to begin.

It wasn't possible to forget Angie's presence, so Hannah reframed it. Folding her body in readiness to dive, she decided that Angie being here was a good omen. Throughout her early swimming career, she was the person against whom she measured herself. Hannah had been a winner then, and she would be now.

She anticipated the starting gun, every muscle primed. When it sounded, she flew into the pool, her feet leaving the block in a perfectly executed movement.

The water cradled her body. There was nothing she loved more than being weightless like this, in the quiet. She followed the black line beneath her, only dimly aware of the swimmer in the next lane. There was no room for thoughts of anything but her own pace. She was conserving energy during this lap, adhering to the race strategy she'd worked out with her coach.

At the first turn, she kicked powerfully against the wall. The chase was what she'd missed, the sense of racing against herself. She worked with the water, letting it propel her forward.

During the last length, her kicking legs burned. She pushed through the pain, shoving it into the background. It was white noise; only static.

She was going to win this race. She *had* to win this race. She was going to win.

When she touched the wall, she bobbed out of the water and sucked in air. Instead of looking around at the other lanes, she swiveled her head to wait for numbers to appear on the board.

She pushed the goggles back onto her cap, squinting to make sure. She rose up in the water, holding out a fist to the roar of the crowd.

Reaching across the lane divider, she hugged Rachel Willis, who'd placed second. Rachel grinned toothily at her, and Hannah was glad they'd just become teammates. She'd have to remember to ask someone exactly how old Rachel was; she must be only sixteen or so. Not much older than Hannah when she'd met Angie.

Hannah hauled herself out of the water and looked for Angie, who nodded toward her.

On shaky legs, Hannah approached her coach, Neil. His stubbly cheek scratched against her as they hugged. They'd worked so hard together, and if not for him agreeing to take her on, she would never have done this.

Neil was the kind of coach who took care of her head and her heart, instead of reducing her to a machine. From the beginning, he'd supported her wishes to concentrate on only the two-hundred-meter race.

"So proud of you, Hannah," he said, slapping her on the back.

Dutifully, Hannah kept her stance opened when the media approached her.

A blond reporter frowned at her, pointing a microphone toward her mouth. "What are you feeling right now? It must be a relief to know that all your hard work has paid off?"

"It is," Hannah said, still trying to regain her breath. There was always a moment when she felt like saying the first thing that jumped into her mind, but she stuck to the stock phrases she'd rehearsed. "It was a very competitive field, and everyone swam their hearts out. I'm very proud that I'll be representing Australia at the Games."

A balding man edged forward, shoving his microphone closer. "You've never talked much about why you left the sport all those years ago. Is that something you'd care to comment on now?"

She forced her smile wider. "I'm sorry I can't help you with that, but there's not much more to say. I felt that I was too young to cope with the demands. I wanted to live a little before I came back. That's all."

As she warmed down with slow strokes, the meaning of the last hour caught up with her. For most of the other women in her race, the journey was at its end. It could have been her. And though there was still so far to go, she allowed herself a precious moment to soak up the fact that it wasn't.

She toweled off next to the warm down pool and started toward the changing rooms, planning on taking a shower to collect herself before the full press conference. Someone stepped in front of her, the two of them narrowly avoiding a collision.

"I'm sorry," Angie said. Hannah's hands came to Angie's shoulders to steady her, but she dropped them quickly.

Angie tipped forward on her toes like she was about to offer a hug. Instead, she put out a hand, painted black nails pointing toward Hannah. Green eyes stood out against her olive skin. "Congratulations, Hannah."

Flashbulbs and shutters popped around them. It was a golden photo opportunity, former Olympic rivals meeting years later.

"Thanks. I have to say, it's funny to see you in Australian colors," Hannah said.

Angie looked down at her green and gold polo shirt. "I know. But I'm proud to be part of the team."

"Right. Anyway, I should…"

"Just a second," Angie said with her palm on Hannah's forearm. When Hannah looked down at it, Angie took it away. "I just wanted to ask you. Maybe we could get breakfast or something? Get caught up? I'm staying over in Bondi, but I'll be here for another week. I'm sure you're busy, but…"

"Thank you for the offer, but I'm not here for long. And you're right, things are pretty frantic right now."

Angie pushed her hair behind her ear, her smile faltering. "Of course, I understand. If it's all right, I'm just going to give you my card. It has my email on it. In case you happen to get some free time…"

She reached into the pocket of her black pants, toying with the card before handing it over. Hannah dampened it as she clutched it between her fingers.

"Imagine how different things would have been if we'd had email back then. It's a pretty crazy invention when you think about it. Like something out of science fiction. Well, it's nice to see you. And again, congratulations."

When Angie dropped her voice and leaned closer, she bent to hear her.

"I know we're not supposed to favor anyone, but I was rooting for you."

"Thanks, Angie."

They stood in place, staring at one another.

It was another thing that hadn't changed. Angie had a way of making Hannah feel important with her kind words, well-placed looks, and touches.

It was what made it so hard to accept how thoughtless she could be.

From behind Angie, another reporter advanced. Hannah was sure that she and Angie would be roped into a joint interview sometime, but it didn't have to be right now. "Excuse me, I should get ready. I'll see you later."

She walked away, pushing her fingers under her swimming cap to draw it off, wincing when it caught on her hair. She was anxious to get through the press conference so she could be away from the attention. All she wanted was a large meal in front of the television.

As she rinsed off, she wondered how she appeared to Angie. The girl she'd been at fourteen was so far away. She had been so unsure of herself back then and desperate for Angie's approval.

Though Angie had been nothing but respectful toward her just now, her presence made Hannah feel small.

Maybe the wounds had never really healed, and she'd just patched them up enough to forget for a little while how painful it had all been.

Hannah scrubbed her skin, hard. None of it mattered. There was too much at stake for her to wallow. She needed to bend her mind toward the idea that having Angie around was a good thing. If she'd learned anything at all from the association with her old rival, it was that swimming was a psychological game.

When you wanted to win, you had to keep your eyes firmly on the prize regardless of what it cost.

CHAPTER TWO

1986 World Aquatic Championships - Madrid

Hannah pushed her tray along the silver countertop. The line moved sluggishly as athletes agonized over what to put on their plates. Most of them were probably being haunted by the voices of their nutritionists right now or imagining being pinched with skinfold tests.

She eyed the piles of fish, rice, salad, vegetables, bread, and steaks. Though the dining hall was set up like a school cafeteria, the food rivaled what you'd find at an all-you-can-eat buffet.

When she reached the front of the line, she heaped steamed vegetables and skinless chicken on her plate. As she scanned the room for an empty table, there was a tap on her shoulder. A girl with light brown hair in a white T-shirt with a large Adidas logo on the front looked back at her. They had seen one another around, but Hannah didn't know this girl's name.

She took her headphones off and rested them around her neck, to acknowledge the girl.

"Hey! I'm Angie. Want to sit together?"

"Hannah. Um…sure?"

She trailed behind Angie, who walked purposefully to a table in the corner. She could tell by Angie's accent that she was American. Hannah wasn't sure why someone from another team was talking to her. Was this girl trying to psych her out?

She slid into the bench seat opposite Angie and turned her music off. There was a Walkman clipped to the waistband of her jeans, and she'd been able to hear tinny music from the headphones while she walked.

"What are you listening to?" Angie said, cutting into a slab of rare steak, pink flesh opening under her knife.

"Joy Division."

"Cool. So, I thought it would be fun to hang out together, you know seeing as we're probably the youngest swimmers here?"

"How old are you?" Hannah replied.

"Fifteen. You're fourteen, right? Coach told me."

"Uh-huh."

Hannah would have pegged her for older than fifteen. With that clear skin and her even, white teeth, Angie would fit in on one of those American TV shows where everyone looked perfect and shiny, like *Growing Pains* or *Family Ties*.

"It's weird being so far away from home, isn't it? My folks are staying at a hotel. Are yours here too?"

Hannah shook her head. Her mother and Paul wanted to come, but the overseas travel was too expensive. She told them not to worry because she'd be so busy with the competition anyway. Since being here, she missed her parents more than she'd imagined she would. It wasn't like being at a sleepover; she couldn't call them to collect her when she grew homesick.

"You won the semifinal in the two hundred today, didn't you?" Angie said.

"I did, yeah."

"You shooting for Seoul? Like, I mean, you want to compete at the Olympics, don't you?"

"Sure, I'll see how it goes."

It was what everyone expected of her, but it was almost two years away. "Do you want to go?"

"Of course! I love your accent, by the way. It's so cool."

"Thanks," she said, although she'd never even thought of herself as having an accent.

In the same instant they each turned to a table behind them. A group of swimmers from the Australian team chanted Tony's name, getting louder with every repetition. A couple of the boys slapped their hands down on the table in time with the sound.

"Who the hell is Tony?" Angie asked.

"The one with the red hair and freckles."

"Oh. Why are they doing that?"

"I really don't know."

"Are they teasing him about something?"

Tony was standing now, laughing with his shorts slung low around his waist. This morning at breakfast Hannah caught him staring at her chest and whispering in Greg's ear. Greg was quiet, but Tony never stopped talking, mainly to brag about his endorsements and interview requests. Greg and Tony were both seventeen and joined at the hip.

"I guess so. The team is always teasing someone about something. Or they probably gave him a dare or whatever."

Angie rolled her eyes. "It's the same with my team. I get so sick of the team spirit, rah rah, rah. It's annoying."

"It bothers you too?"

"Of course. And I get so tired of being treated like a kid. They're not that much older than me."

"Same here."

Most of her teammates had been swimming seriously for years, and some of them had already been to the Olympics. Whenever she won a race, she braced herself for the subtle frostiness that came her way. Nobody had explained it to her, but she supposed she hadn't paid her dues or earned her place.

"You know, I don't see why I should be friends with people just because they're from the same country as me. Sometimes people from other teams are just as nice," Angie said.

Eyes met across the table as they smiled. Angie's green eyes were pretty, framed by long lashes.

Hannah shrugged. "Maybe we could eat together again tomorrow. If you wanted to, I mean."

"Sure. We could do that. Right after I whip you," Angie said.

"What?"

"I won my semifinal too. I'm racing you tomorrow morning."

"Oh."

It was over before it had begun. Even if she didn't beat Angie, competing against one another would make it weird.

Angie kicked her leg under the table. "Don't look so worried! It's not a problem. I know you'll beat me, but I don't mind."

"Maybe I won't?"

"I bet you will. If you win, I get to make you eat whatever I want when we have dinner tomorrow night. It's like a dare."

"Why would I want to win if I have to eat something gross?" Hannah said. With anyone else, she'd assume they were laying a trap, but Angie's dancing eyes made her sure that everything was okay.

"It'll make the loser feel better. If I place before you, you can make me eat whatever you want. For the record, I don't like tomato, ugh," Angie said, the point of her tongue sticking out. "So, if you wanted to mess with me, that's what you can pick. Now your turn."

"I don't eat red meat. I'd be vegetarian if I could, but my nutritionist says it's a bad idea for me right now. I wouldn't get enough fuel or something."

Angie leaned over to slap her arm. "I'm not going to make you eat a steak! Jeez, what do you think I am? Pick something less mean."

"All right…I guess I don't like broccoli?"

"Thanks for the tip," Angie said, and they shook on it.

The following morning Hannah's pulse hammered as she entered the marshaling area. The crowd bore down on her, bigger than it was for semifinals. The high stakes made her breath catch in her throat.

Her gaze fell on Angie, who was staring back at her and wiggling her eyebrows. How could she joke around at a time like this?

They entered the pool deck, Hannah averting her eyes from the bleachers and cameras. It was always so strange to stand in front of a crowd in her bathers. Sometimes she felt like her body wasn't her own. It belonged to her coach, her trainer, and anyone else who wanted a piece of it. She'd shot up over the past year. She was taller than a lot of the boys now, and her shoulders were broader than a lot of girls'.

The thought of the dare almost made her smile. She hoped that either she or Angie would win so they could have fun at dinner. Maybe she should have suggested something to do if neither of them placed. She was still thinking about it when the gun went off, and then she was in the water.

The last two years boiled down to the stroke of her arms and her hands slicing through the water. All the kilometers she'd swum before and after school, struggling along in a weighted vest. The time spent at the gym working on strengthening her core, endless advice from nutritionists, race strategy talk so dull it made her eyes glaze over.

When she started swimming it had been just for fun. In increments, she'd discovered that when it came to this, she was special. She loved being in the water, but she didn't like that people treated her differently because of it.

Her turn wasn't as graceful as she wanted it to be, but she gained some ground in the second lap. She was almost a full body length ahead of the swimmer beside her. The next time she turned it was perfect, and she drove harder, giving all that she had. She forgot about everything, the dare far from her mind for the first time since the night before.

She knew she'd won before she touched the wall. She sought out Angie, breathing hard a couple of lanes away. Angie's expression betrayed only a hint of disappointment at coming in second, and then she smiled. When they were out of the water, Angie gave her a quick hug, her arms slick around Hannah's shoulders.

On the dais, they faced straight ahead in their sweatpants and zipped up coats, Hannah's arms pressed against her sides. It was her first gold, and she wondered if her parents would put it on top of the bookshelf with her brothers' football trophies. Over the past few years, she'd amassed a pile of ribbons and trophies. She liked that her parents didn't act like she was special; she was the same as her siblings in their eyes.

When the national anthem played she pulled her arms more tightly against herself, trying not to scratch her face or fidget.

"I hope I can find some little trees for you tonight," Angie cracked as they stepped down from the dais.

Later, Hannah stared at the picture that was taken immediately after Angie said that. Only she knew that the mile-wide grin spread across her face was because of something other than winning.

Hannah had never been involved in a press conference this big. She was seated at a long table, set up in front of rows of chairs. She was a rabbit caught in the headlights, frozen in front of the cameramen clustered in the back of the room. She tried to swallow, and Angie pushed a glass of water toward her. The moment of eye contact they shared steadied her.

A young reporter with a shaved head asked the first question, and his peers burst into laughter. Hannah looked toward the translator, jogging her leg while she waited to understand.

"How do you have time for all the things teenage girls usually like, such as boys and clothes?"

Hannah took another sip of water. She cut her gaze across to Angie, who was sitting back from her microphone, letting Hannah go first.

"The most important things to me are swimming and school. Everything else comes second," Hannah said.

The man who'd asked the question nodded politely. Angie finally bent her head toward the microphone. "But we're both good multi-taskers. Training is important, but I'd go nuts if I couldn't go shopping once in a while."

The audience laughed again. For the rest of the press conference, Hannah let Angie go first unless the question was explicitly addressed to her. When they were done and being ushered away from the press room by an official, she leaned toward Angie.

"You're so much better at this part than I am."

"Not even," Angie said. "You're all cool and quiet; it makes you seem mysterious. My folks made me go to this silly media training thing. I'll give you tips if you want, but who cares?"

"Right," Hannah said. Her coach had sent her to media training too, but the lessons were forgotten as soon as she was in front of a crowd.

"Are you leaving tomorrow?" Angie asked, looping their arms together.

"Yep," Hannah said. It wasn't fair that they only had one more night to get to know one another.

"Well then, I dare you to stay up hanging out with me all night."

"You're on."

CHAPTER THREE

2000 - Sydney

Hannah threw back the covers and checked the clock on the nightstand. The red numbers told her that it was nine thirty. There was no point going to bed early if she was going to lie here torturing herself, instead of falling into her typical exhausted sleep.

The ocean was a ten-minute walk away. The sound of crashing waves was one of the many things she loved about staying in Bondi. The thought of being close to the water comforted her, so she got up and pulled on jeans that were crumpled up next to the bed, with a blue T-shirt. She slid her feet into the flip-flops she kept beside the front door, still sandy from an earlier trip along the shoreline.

It was a relief that here, she could come and go without anyone noticing her. The one-bedroom apartment was Debbie's, a friend who was on an overseas business trip. There was stiff competition to secure time at her place; Hannah wasn't the only person with a key. It was cozy and light, large windows lining the curved wall of the living room.

The streets were busy, people wandering around or dining at outdoor tables in the balmy night air. Nobody recognized her as she passed by with her hands stuck in her pockets, her head stooped. She dropped into a late-night café to pick up takeaway hot chocolate, then carried the warm cardboard cup to the beach.

She sat on a wooden bench that gave her a panoramic view of the dark waves. She watched them, finally allowing herself to think about what had kept her awake. Now that she'd attained her goal, her mantra was transformed. All she could think about was Angie slipping her that card after the trial. When Hannah arrived back at Debbie's apartment, she carelessly threw it on the coffee table to prove to herself that she wasn't going to use it.

Now, the mantra was that she needed to see Angie. She *had* to see her. It was hard to pin down exactly what she wanted to get out of meeting with her, but now that the opportunity had presented itself, she was going to grab it with both hands.

She jumped up from the bench and walked away from the shore. Debbie wouldn't mind if she used her computer. When Hannah was back in the apartment, she booted it up and logged into her email account. Good old-fashioned paper mail was better, the licking of stamps and the movement of a pen across the page. Still, she had to admit that email had its benefits. The speed of it meant she might even be able to see Angie before going back to Melbourne. She pecked at the keyboard with two fingers, trying to strike the right tone.

Hi Angie. It turns out my plans have changed, and I have tomorrow morning free if you see this in time. I thought it might be good to meet like you suggested. I'm staying at a friend's apartment in Bondi. Maybe you could come over here for a cup of coffee or something around 11?

She switched to the Internet browser and opened a window, searching Angie's name. Now that she'd pried open the lid from Pandora's box, she couldn't stop herself. A page with pictures from a recent event loaded. There was Angie, her toned shoulders and smooth skin revealed in her red dress. When Hannah found herself staring at Angie's low neckline, she rushed to close the window.

She was moving the mouse to log out of her email account when she saw that Angie had already replied.

Sounds great! I'm free whenever! It's so cool that you're staying here too. I wonder if you're close by. That would be funny. Send me your address and the time you can see me, and I'll be there. It's been so lovely to see you again. I've missed you. - A.

She pushed her finger down hard on the mouse. If Angie missed her, whose fault was that? She took a deep breath before composing a reply.

The next morning she checked the shelves in Debbie's pantry, finding only corn flakes and a package of noodles. There was a market across the street, so she crossed over to gather supplies. At the checkout she unloaded two types of coffee, fruit, a package of crackers, hummus, celery, and carrot.

When she got back to the apartment she sliced watermelon into wedges and rinsed grapes. She fluffed the cushions on the sofa and paced around until there was a knock at the door.

Angie stood in the doorway, casual in a denim skirt with a white button-up shirt. She wore brown leather sandals, which showed her black toenails that matched her manicure.

"Hey," Hannah said, eyeing the bouquet of roses Angie held in front of her.

"Hello," Angie said. "I wanted to congratulate you."

"Oh. Thank you," she replied, taking the bundle from her. "I guess I'll find somewhere to put these. Come in."

Hannah stuffed the bunch into a large water glass. Angie was tilting her head, taking in a photograph of Debbie with her parents' German shepherd on the mantelpiece.

"Can I get you some coffee?" Hannah asked, brushing stray hair behind her ear. She'd tied it half-back and applied makeup, but she'd worn only jeans and a white T-shirt. Like throwing the card on the coffee table, it was a useless gesture. A way of trying to fool herself into believing that she didn't care for Angie's opinion of how she looked.

"That would be great. Thanks. This is a really nice place, super nice. I love the windows; they give such a great view. It was close like I thought it might be, just around the corner from my hotel if you can believe it. I really like this area. I went for a walk to the beach this morning. I even saw the sunrise. I didn't get into the water, but it was nice to see the surfers and everything. Those waves are really something else. So...How long are you staying?"

"I fly out early tomorrow morning."

"Oh," Angie said. She glanced at the roses, which were dropping their petals onto the table.

"What about you?" Hannah said, taking two mugs from where they hung on hooks above the countertop. "Help yourself to some fruit if you want."

Angie walked over to the table where Hannah had laid a platter. She snapped some grapes from their cluster, her stare darting around the apartment.

"I'll be staying here another few days. I haven't spent much time in Sydney, so I'm looking forward to checking the place out. I was thinking I'd go to the opera house tomorrow, see the bridge and all that stuff. Someone told me I should take a ferry as well. Whose place is this?" she asked, the words bursting forth quickly.

"It's my friend Debbie's. She's letting me stay here while I'm in town. She's in Japan right now for work. You probably don't remember but you met her once."

She approached Angie with the steaming coffee mug. When Angie took it from her, Hannah thought she saw a brightly colored watch flashing under her white top, but she pulled the sleeve down before she could get a good view of it.

"Of course, I remember her. Nice girl. I'm sorry, I didn't mean to pry or anything."

"It's fine. Do you want to sit down?"

The cream-colored sofa under the window was Hannah's favorite piece of furniture in the apartment. The previous owners had it custom made to fit the curved shape of the wall, and they let Debbie keep it when she took over the lease.

Leaving space between them, Hannah curled her hands around her mug and blew on the top. Angie stared out the window, head tilted away, but Hannah could still see her eyes. She had forgotten how they changed in the light; they were as blue-green as the ocean now.

When she finally turned back, her gaze drifted over Hannah, who crossed her arms. "You're just the same, you know."

"Is that so?"

"I mean it as a compliment. You look great. And you seem…I don't know how to put it. You knew yourself and who you were when we were teenagers much better than I did, and you still seem like that."

"Really," Hannah said flatly.

Angie looked out of the window again. "Okay. I guess I just wanted to say that I didn't know you were planning a return until after I'd agreed to join the coaching team. I'd heard rumors that you were training, but I didn't know for sure."

"You don't have to explain yourself to me, but thank you. You know, we were just teenagers. There's no need for us to make a big deal out of anything."

"Right, of course. What made you want to come back, anyway? I mean, I always hoped that you would. I thought it was such a shame that you retired so young when you had so much to offer. You could have gone to another Games back then, maybe even made it to three in a row. Or four because you started so young. It never seemed fair to me. You achieved a lot, more than most people could ever hope for, but still."

Hannah sat cross-legged, making a fist and resting her chin on it. "I don't have a simple answer to that."

"I'm not in a rush. I'd like to hear it," Angie said, her voice soft. "In case you didn't hear, I retired after '96 in Atlanta, and it kind of sucked. I don't get too many chances to talk to people who understand what it was like, or what it was like to give it up. That's why I've missed our letters and everything. I bet you don't get a chance to talk to people about it too much either."

"That's true. But I mean, there's no one thing that made me give it up. My coach had a lot to do with it but that wasn't everything. You know what I could never wrap my head around, though?"

"What's that?" Angie said.

"That I was making more money than my parents just for swimming up and down in a pool. Like, does it ever seem crazy to you that we had so much thrown at us, just for that?"

Angie narrowed her eyes. "Hannah, are you kidding? We didn't just swim up and down in a pool. We worked our asses off. We were just kids, but we worked longer hours than a lot of adults do. All that pressure too!"

"You know what I mean, though. Right? The more I think about it, the more I believe it's a stupid way to earn a living. That's why I can come back now, because it's not my whole life."

"But you *love* it. You love being in the water. So what if it was your whole life? What's wrong with that?"

Hannah laughed. "Well, yeah. You're right, I came back because I do love it. I think I just needed to grow into it. It was all too much, everything about it. If I had my way, there would be an age restriction on when you can start swimming professionally."

"Is that why you ended up being a teacher and swim coach? You wanted to make sure other kids didn't have to go through the same stuff as we did?"

"I suppose that had something to do with it, yeah," Hannah said. There was no need to ask how Angie knew about her job. No doubt she'd seen it in the media.

"Well, I guess I learned something from it all too. I've made it one of my priorities to look after the wellbeing of the younger kids on the team. Like Rachel, she's only sixteen. I'll make sure I keep an eye on her."

"Good. Rachel is so young," Hannah said. She rested her mug on the windowsill then followed the line of Angie's sight to the street below. A couple strode along the sidewalk arm-in-arm, two short-haired women with their heads bowed close together.

Angie slowly put her mug down next to Hannah's. "I should let you rest. I'm sure you're tired after the last few days."

"Not so tired. It's not like I can sleep in the middle of the day, like you. I always wondered how you could drop off like that."

Angie stared back at her, nodding slowly. "Just lucky, I guess. Listen, would you mind if I emailed you again? To keep in touch, I mean?"

"Sure, you can email me if you want."

She walked Angie to the door, opening it for her. They approached one another at the same time, Angie's arms encircling her.

The fragrance of Angie's hair was overwhelming. Hannah closed her eyes, breathing in before they each pulled away. How could it be that the past was flooding back to her so quickly?

"I'll see you," Angie said, a small smile on her lips as the door closed behind her.

CHAPTER FOUR

1987 – Melbourne

"Hannah? Are you with us?"

Hannah slid her elbow to cover her spiral notebook. Mr. Cochran was in front of the blackboard with chalk between his fingers, pointing it at her. He liked calling on her when he could see that she wasn't listening, gaining a look of sly satisfaction when he caught her out.

"Yes, Mr. Cochran."

He faced the blackboard, thick black hair curling around his shirt collar. "Sorry if it's boring for you, being in class now that you're a world champion."

Her classmates giggled and she crossed her legs the other way, looking back down at her notebook. There were block letters scrawled across the page. She filled in black lines along the edges to give the letters a shadow, then wrapped a cartoon banner around it. Mr. Cochran droned on about the central nervous system, then clapped his hands together once.

"All right class, get into pairs, please, and I want you to do the exercise on page fifteen."

"What does that mean? B-O-H-J-F? I don't get it," Marie said, tilting Hannah's notebook toward her. When she leaned over, she pushed back her black corkscrew curls. Marie wanted straight hair like hers, and she always told her she'd be more than happy to swap.

Hannah turned the page, smoothing her palm over the next page. She'd pressed down hard enough to leave deep indents on the paper. "Nothing, just doodling. Should we do the question?"

"Nah. Mr. Cochran's being a real dickhead today," Marie said, taking a tube of eyeliner from her backpack and unscrewing the lid. She'd started wearing makeup as soon as they got into high school.

"It's okay. It's not like he's the first teacher to treat me differently since I got back," she said.

"He's just jealous because he's a loser. Have you seen his wife? I'm afraid of what their kids are going to look like, especially when he looks like a primate. Me and Debbie are going over to her place after school. Do you want to come?" she asked, snapping her compact closed.

"Got to get to training like I do every day, dummy. Thanks for inviting me, anyway."

The bell rang and Mr. Cochran looked directly at Hannah. "I hope you were all doing what I asked. I'm going to ask for your answers to that question next class."

She stuffed her notebook into her backpack, saying a quick goodbye to Marie. Her mom's white station wagon idled on the street in front of the school entrance, and she ran over to it, sliding into the passenger seat. A moment after she'd leaned over to kiss her mother's cheek, her two brothers jumped into the car. They were lanky mirror images of one another, shouting goodbye to their friends out of the open window.

"Can we stop at the video shop on the way? We want to get that movie about that guy that turns into a fly. Dave saw it and he said it's awesome," Mark said. He leaned forward so that his head was between the front seats, jet-black hair flopping over an eye.

"We can stop after we've taken Hannah to her training," their mother said, frowning in concentration as she changed lanes. There were dark smudges around her hairline. She cut her hair short and dyed it herself because she couldn't stand the small talk at the salon. Mom liked doing everything differently from other people, and she asked them to call her by her first name, Viv. "And you can watch it after you've cleaned your room."

"Can't we go there first and you take us home before you go? We could watch half the movie in the time it'll take to do all that," Ethan whined.

"You can just wait, Ethan-or-Mark," Hannah said. She'd never had trouble telling the twins apart but calling them by their shared school nickname got under their skin.

"Bitch," Mark said, his voice cracking. She bit her tongue because Viv had asked her not to mention it. The light hair growing above his top lip was off-limits too.

"Mark! Don't talk to your sister like that or we're not stopping at the video shop at all. Hannah, you got a letter today. I think it's from your American friend," Viv said, eyes darting to the rearview mirror.

"Did you bring it?" Hannah asked.

"I left it on your desk. Ethan, I can see you! Don't punch your brother."

In the pool, Hannah's stroke was precise lap after lap. She wished Viv had brought the letter so she could read it on the ride over, but at least now there was something to look forward to. She gave herself over to memories of Angie and smiled into the water.

That night at dinner after they'd raced one another in the finals, Angie presented her with a plate of chicken and vegetables. She laughed at the tiny broccoli floret on a napkin at the side of the tray and ate it first.

Because Angie's roommate had already left to stay in a motel with her family, they spent the night in Angie's room. They talked until dawn, splayed out on the single bed, eating contraband chocolate given to Angie by a teammate. Angie's gaze snagged on her when she thought something Hannah said was funny, which was way more often than anyone else seemed to think.

"It's so shitty that you live so far away. Do you think we could be pen pals?" Angie asked in the morning, yawning. "It's so nice to have someone I can talk to about all this stuff for a change."

"Sure. If you want to."

"Of course, I want to! And can we hang out next time we have a competition too?"

"Sure, I guess," Hannah said, grinning when Angie punched her in the arm.

When practice was over Hannah changed quickly, knowing that her stepdad Paul would be waiting for her outside. As soon as she got home, she ran toward her room.

"Hannah! Make sure you take your gear out of your bag today. I don't want to find another bag of stinky clothes in your room!" Viv called from the kitchen.

Snatching up the envelope from her desk, she took a moment to linger over her name written in Angie's hand. She ran a fingertip over the swirls and hearts drawn along the edges.

As she tore open her prize, she moved onto the bed and settled against the pillows. Photos fell onto the mattress beside her. There were two pictures of Angie, surrounded by powder-blue sky and mountains. She looked so cool, wearing acid-washed jeans and a shirt covered in palm trees.

Dear H,

How are you? I am fine. I laughed so much at your last letter. Thanks for the photos. It's so funny to me that your school uniform has that purple stripe across the front. It's not like any uniforms I've seen here. We can wear whatever we want to school. You look cute in yours. You've probably seen them by now but the photos are from when we went to Yosemite last summer. It was the best day.

I'm writing this to you on Sunday afternoon, no training today. So I've been hanging out with Trace, Joe and Rachel. We went to the movies and the mall. You know how you said about how sometimes you feel lonely even when you're with your friends? I think I know what you mean. I had fun today, but I wished you were there too. I hope I don't sound weird.

Anyways I have some big news. Sorry I kept you in suspense until now, but Dad is coming to Melbourne on business, and they say that if I promise to keep up my training regime for a couple of weeks while I'm there, I can come with him. I told them I could probably go to the same pool as you and get like a program or something from coach to work on while I was there and we could motivate each other.

What do you think? Let me know. He's coming in July. Maybe write me back a letter and tell me what you think and if you have time with school and training and everything. Then I'll call you to work out the details if the answer is yes. But like I said we could train together. Maybe we can have a bet again. More broccoli for you!

Lots of love, -A.

Hannah squeezed the letter against her chest. Angie would be here for two full weeks, as part of her world. Angie would be here and that made the whole world burst into color.

For the next two months, their letters were filled with a passionate discussion about the visit. Hannah wanted to think only about the fact that Angie was coming. Things had changed so much since the world championships, and her connection to Angie was one of the few constants in her life.

Requests and invitations were pouring in. A cereal company wanted her to represent them. She was asked to give a speech at an event at the exhibition center, and the state tourism board wanted her for their new advertising campaign. The weirdest thing of all was when producers from Channel Eight asked if she was interested in a guest role on *Reef's Edge*. It was one of the country's biggest nightly soaps; Marie loved it. It took all of ten seconds for Hannah to shoot down that offer.

"What about this one?" Viv said, pushing a notepad across the table. There were red splashes on the corner of the page from the pasta sauce she'd been making when she scribbled down the message.

"Fishermen? I love them!" she said. A few of the kids at school had the unique wristwatches, each of them with a different design but the same chunky band and large face. She tapped the paper with a finger. "I want to do this. Let's book it."

"Are you sure?" Viv asked, screwing up her face. "This is for an ad. You haven't been too keen on doing photo shoots and things like that."

"What if they give me a free watch, though?"

"Hannah! You can't do something just for a free watch. We can get you one for Christmas if you're so desperate for a watch."

"I think it would be cool."

"If it's what you really want…"

Three weeks later Hannah stood before an array of Fishermen watches, bands in every style and color. The representative told her that she could select any two she would like to keep, smiling down indulgently at her. Viv clasped her hand while Hannah bit her lip, pointing hesitatingly to one and then another. The best watch's band was aqua and decorated with mermaids, their flame-colored hair billowing behind them.

The next day at school, she was sitting with Marie at lunch when Scott, the boy Marie was dating, came over. The watch caught his eye, and Scott pointed to it, snorting.

"Those mermaids supposed to be you on that watch or something? Got a picture of yourself swimming around? The hair is the wrong color, but otherwise, she's a dead ringer for you."

Hannah crossed her arms, pushing her wrist under her elbow to hide it from view.

But the shame didn't last for long, because when she got home after training, a letter from Angie waited. Her mom had propped the envelope against the vase in the center of the dining table.

Dear Hannah,

Is it just me or is this time going on forever and ever? But like, in a way I don't want to come see you because then it will be over. And I don't know when I'll get to see you again, which makes me totally sad.

I'm trying to be more positive about it. We'll still get to see each other at competitions, and it can be like that night in Madrid. We'll just stay up late and smoosh as much as we can into the time we get to be in the same place. I have been thinking about all the things I want to say when I see you, and it makes me feel so nervous and happy at the same time.

It was funny when you said you were worried I wouldn't like you when I spent more time with you! I already feel like I know you so well just from that night and from our letters, too. You shouldn't worry so much.

Congratulations on your endorsement deal! I bet you look awesome in the pictures and I can't wait to see them. Thanks for putting in the photo of your watch. It's very cool. I know what you mean. I feel uncomfortable having my picture taken by strangers as well. As for me, I've been doing some interviews and stuff. I've been working with that swimwear company I was telling you about. It's so annoying, but my parents are so happy about it you'd think I was working for NASA or something.

P.S. Did you ever notice that your name is the same way spelled forward and backward?

Love, -A.

CHAPTER FIVE

Hannah and Angie sat on the edge of the pool, swinging their legs back and forth in the water. In the shallow end, a teacher wrangled children into paying attention to their swimming lesson. Their happy screams and splashes echoed off the walls.

"It's so weird to come here and have it be so cold outside! Right in the middle of my summer," Angie said, wiping water from her face. "And then it's so warm in here."

"I know. It must be weird. Who won that one, anyway? I couldn't tell, and it felt like maybe it was a tie."

Angie shrugged. "I'm not sure. I think we both did pretty good, don't you?"

"Absolutely."

All morning they'd been chasing each other up and down the pool and fooling around in between laps. They competed to see who could hold their breath for the longest, submerged and sitting on the bottom. Angie said it was a legitimate training technique because they were testing their lung capacity. It turned into an underwater screaming match, the two of them yelling swear words with air bubbling up from their mouths. When they sprang from the surface, they giggled, bobbing again and again.

Before Angie arrived, Hannah asked Viv to tell her coach that she was taking a short break from their sessions. Viv was given strict instructions not to mention Angie, to only say that Hannah would be training independently for a couple of weeks. Tim would hit the roof if he knew she was training with a rival. She gathered that Tim wasn't happy about it, but for her, it was worth whatever anger he might take out on her when they got back to work.

She inspected her legs compared to Angie's. The whiteness of her thighs reflected that she hadn't been in the sun for a long time, but Angie's skin was a warm tan. Her navy-blue swimsuit was the perfect cut for her. Hannah begged her parents to get her a new suit in time for the visit, but the black one she'd chosen wasn't as flattering as Angie's.

"It's so cool of your folks to let you have time off from school while I'm here," Angie said.

"It's not so long. Our school holiday starts on Friday anyway," Hannah replied. "My folks were glad for me to get a break. They worry about me balancing everything, especially my mom. She worries a lot. She doesn't want me to get stressed out."

"You're lucky. My parents would never let me do something like that. They're always at me to keep my grades up, saying they don't want me just to be a jock and everything," Angie said, removing her swimming cap and twisting her ponytail to wring it out. "I can't wait to finish school. I'm going to be done with it as soon as I can."

"I wish I could drop out of school. I'd miss being around my friends, but everyone's treating me like I'm a weirdo or something."

Angie dropped her hand into the water and splashed Hannah, who squeezed her eyes shut. "Screw them. You're better than all of them."

"That's what Viv says."

"Then listen to her. She knows what she's talking about. She and Paul are so nice. It's so great to be at your house; I love it."

"I know it's small, but it's close to everything. I can't believe your dad was going to book a separate hotel room for you! That's crazy."

"Yeah, he likes to have his own space. I hate sharing with him too; he snores like a drain. I bet he's glad I'm here. Last time I went on a business trip with him I ordered so much room service because I got bored. I ate all the potato chips that were in the mini-bar too. He flipped out when it was time to settle, and he saw what I'd done."

"Must have been fun, though. Hey, I have an idea. Let's wag training tomorrow and do something fun. All we've done is swim since you got here. What if we just jumped on a train and went somewhere? Would you want to do that?"

"Huh? What does wag mean?"

"Like…skip it. Like you'd wag school."

"Oh, play hooky? This is like when you called your swimsuit 'togs,'" Angie said, kicking her leg. "You Aussies are so weird."

Hannah kicked back, clutching the pool's edge. "The way we talk is normal. It's you guys that are weird."

When Angie put her hand down on the concrete ledge next to Hannah's their fingers touched. "Okay, whatever you say. It's a good idea about tomorrow. That sounds super fun."

For the first time, Hannah was happy that their terrace house was too small to have a spare room. It was as long and thin as a train carriage, the bedrooms branching off from the hall. Mark and Ethan shared the largest room at the front of the house.

Before Angie arrived, Hannah and Viv pulled a single mattress into her bedroom and made it up with white flannel sheets. There was barely room to walk around it, but it made the room cozy.

Each night Hannah and Angie stayed awake until late, their bodies slack from training but their mouths racing to keep pace with the conversation.

In some ways, it was like having Debbie or Marie over. But with them, Hannah never had the tripping heartbeat or the keen awareness of her own body under the sheets. A tone in Angie's voice struck a chord in Hannah, making her wriggle on her mattress like a worm on a hook.

In the morning she rolled onto her side to see Angie looking back at her, her skin creased with sleep.

"Mmmm. Morning," she said, rubbing a hand over her face. She quickly wiped around her mouth and checked the corners of her eyes.

"What are we doing today? Going to the movies or something like that?"

"I think we can do better than that. How do you feel about amusement parks? We should go to Luna Park. It's a little one over in St. Kilda, by the beach. What do you think?"

Angie leaped from her mattress, jumping onto Hannah's bed and throwing her arms around her neck. "Does this answer your question?"

"Don't get so excited; it's not the greatest place on earth or anything!" she said, wishing they could stay like this forever.

On the way to the park on the tram, Hannah watched Angie pressing her face to the window, taking in the Melbourne streets as they slipped by, trying to ignore it when an older man with a mustache recognized them. He leaned forward on his seat until Hannah was sure he was going to say something. She looked down at her hands, wishing people wouldn't stare so much.

They stepped down from the tram, the bell ringing to clear its path. A chill wind from the nearby beach blew their hair back. Together they walked up to the park, to the large white face with painted red lips that arched around the entrance.

"Whoa! That face is kind of creepy," Angie said. "Don't you think?"

"I told you it wasn't that great."

"Are you kidding? It's amazing! I love it. We sure don't have one of these in Austin. Let's go! I want to get on that rollercoaster!"

They rode the white rails around the park, screaming as they whipped past the curves. Hannah hadn't been here for years and hadn't wanted to come when Mark and Ethan had visited a while back, saying that it was for little kids. Sharing it with Angie made everything new. They argued over whether it was called fairy floss or cotton candy and played a ball game. Hannah tried to win a stuffed animal for Angie.

She threw the last ball, swearing when it bounced off her target. "This game is rigged!"

Angie grabbed her wrist. "Hannah, is that a ghost train over there? We have to!"

"How did you know? Was it the big sign that says ghost train?" Hannah said, but she was already following Angie, fishing out the pink paper tokens she'd stuffed into her jeans' pocket.

While they waited in line, they watched carriages slap through the exit doors, disembarking passengers wide-eyed and laughing. A tiny girl with blond hair cried while her mother tugged her along by a balled fist.

Angie bumped Hannah with her shoulder. "That's going to be you in a few minutes. I can tell."

At last, they reached the front of the line. They were strapped into a carriage by a boy who looked only a few years older than them.

Angie put a hand on Hannah's forearm, making her flex her fingers on the steel bar that lay across them. "This is so much fun. Thanks for bringing me. Hanging out with you is making me wish I lived here, you know? Or you lived in America so we could see each other more."

"Me too."

The carriage creaked forward on its tracks until they were inside, discordant organ music wrapping itself around shrieks and cackles. Glowing green lights were peppered in the dark. They rounded a corner, and Angie screamed, swatting at her hair.

"Somebody just touched me!"

A skeleton lurched toward them. Hannah jumped and moved closer to Angie, who grabbed her hand. They pushed through double doors, and a graveyard came into view, a ring of lights around it. A figure sat up and stared at them; there was nothing but black holes for eyes. They screamed, laughed and screamed again. Angie's hand was in hers, their fingers interlaced.

After they left Luna Park, they traveled on the tram to Flinders Street station to catch a connecting train. At dusk, Paul picked them up from the station close to home. They sat on the backseat, Angie's arm flung out so close to her that for a moment, Hannah was sure they were going to hold hands again.

"I guess I'm your cab driver tonight, huh dudes?" Paul said with a tattooed arm draped over the back of the seat and one hand on the wheel. He was five years younger than Viv, and Hannah hated the way he tried to act like her friend. But at least he was kind to her, and he got along well with Mark and Ethan. Viv had a boyfriend before him who hadn't made any effort with them at all.

She shrugged and looked out the window. It hadn't occurred to her that she should sit next to Paul.

"Okay, okay, I get it. Well, did you girls have a good time today?"

"We had so much fun!" Angie exclaimed. "We went on the ghost train twice, did the roller coaster and all that. We had hot dogs and fairy floss. Then we went for a walk along the beach, which was awesome even though it was windy. The park was such a cool little place."

"I'm glad you enjoyed it. So, we all took a vote while you were out and agreed we should introduce you to a good old-fashioned Aussie barbecue tonight. What do you think?"

"Isn't it a bit cold for a barbeque?" Hannah said. She and Angie had talked about making sandwiches for dinner and taking them into her room.

"Oh no, I'd love a barbecue! Thank you," Angie said. She reached across to take Hannah's wrist, turning it over to see the face of her watch. "I love this so much. I love mermaids. It suits you. It's so funny to think it's the middle of the night back home."

When they arrived at the house, they found Viv, Ethan, and Mark in the kitchen. Hannah guessed they had decided to prepare for a barbecue with or without their agreement. Ethan awkwardly chopped onions into rings, his eyes almost closed as he struggled against tears. Viv strained water from potatoes, steam rising from the sink.

"Hi girls! Did you have fun today?"

"We did!" Angie said. "The park was awesome. Especially the ghost train. Can we help with something Viv? I hear we're having a barbecue. I can't wait!"

"I caaaaan't wait!" Mark said in a high-pitched voice.

"You little shit, I told you to stop imitating her accent last night," Hannah said, glaring at him.

"It's cool, mate! Let's not worry about it and enjoy this barbie!" Angie laughed, slinging her arm around Hannah's shoulders.

"Your Aussie accent is terrible," she said.

"Mark, stop doing that, and Hannah, just because he's acting like a little shit doesn't mean you can call him one. And Angie, thank you. If you could set the outdoor table that would be wonderful. Hannah can show you where everything is."

They sat on the back patio to eat. Angie wore one of Hannah's sweaters and a blanket draped around her knees. A row of dishes sat along the table filled with coleslaw, potato salad, fried onion, rissoles, and sausages. Paul put a plate in front of Hannah, with a piece of fish he'd just lifted from the grill. For the first time in months, watching Angie wrap a rissole in soft white bread, Hannah wished she still ate red meat.

"Australian barbecues are awesome," Angie said when their stomachs were full, carrying a stack of plates inside.

"Glad you enjoyed it, love. What do you think, should we watch a movie or something? We've got ice cream?" Viv asked.

"That sounds great, but I'm super tired. Still getting over the jet lag, I guess. I thought I might go to bed soon," Angie said.

When Angie came back from the shower, Hannah was in her bed, staring at nothing. After they'd gotten off the roller coaster, she'd bought a photograph of them coming around the last curve from the nearby stand. The photo was tucked into the shoebox under her bed now, where she kept all of Angie's letters and any photographs she hadn't stuck to the wall.

If she closed her eyes, she could still see the picture, both of them laughing as they screamed with their hands in the air.

"Can I put on some music?" Angie asked. Her pajamas were pastel blue, punctuated by yellow stars and moons.

"Of course, you can, but I thought you were tired?"

Angie flipped through the collection of tapes Hannah kept in a shoebox on her desk. She held up a Joy Division album. "You know I had no idea who these guys were when you mentioned them in Spain? I wrote it down when I got back to my room and asked my dad to buy me this tape. I'm actually not that tired; I just wanted to hang out. But I like hanging out with your family. They're so nice!"

"Except for my brothers."

"Oh, they're not so bad. You're lucky you have them. Only thing I want more than a sister is a little brother."

The opening bars of "Disorder" played while Angie walked over to the light switch. The room fell dark to the sound of the drums and clean guitar notes.

"So…Hannah, do you have a boyfriend or anything?" Angie asked from the floor, her voice closer than usual.

"Nah. Do you?" Hannah said, wetting her lips.

It was a strange question for Angie to ask now, when they'd been writing to one another for months. One of the things Hannah enjoyed about talking with Angie was the fact that boys never came up. Even Marie and Debbie spoke about this stuff more than she'd like, but she had learned to bat that kind of attention away. It was easy to say that she was too busy with swimming to care about boys, and her friends seemed to accept it.

"No. Have you ever had one?"

"Not yet, no. Kind of have my mind on other things," Hannah said.

"Have you had your first kiss yet?"

"What's with all the questions? Are you auditioning to be a journalist or something? You'd fit right in with them, I think. Are you taping me from down there?"

"We just haven't talked about any of this stuff before, that's all."

Hannah rolled onto her side to look down at Angie. "All right, then no I haven't. But I bet you have."

It was only a white lie. There was a party at Marie's house a few months ago, and she kissed a boy called Oliver Blake from her biology class. They were pushed together during a game that Hannah hated, called two minutes in the closet.

Hannah hadn't wanted to play but couldn't think of a way to get out of it without anyone noticing. She was afraid of being called frigid, but then it was awful, the way everyone hooted and clapped when it was her turn to get shut away with Oliver.

Oliver's tongue in her mouth was like a wet slug. It seemed to go on forever as she waited for the time to tick over so the other kids would knock on the door and interrupt them.

"What makes you say you bet I've kissed someone? Do I seem easy or something?" Angie asked.

"Totally. Easy street. I bet you've made out with every dude at your school."

Angie knocked the wind out of her when she jumped on top of her. They shrieked and giggled as Angie held her wrists down on the mattress. "How dare you?"

After a few moments of wrestling, Angie climbed off but stayed close to her side. "I haven't, you know. It makes me feel weird when all my friends have. I mean, except you."

"Well, there you go. Neither of us has. There's nothing wrong with that."

"It would be nice to have it over with, wouldn't it?"

The strip of light spilling in from under the door showed the way Angie stared back at her. Hannah shrugged again. The meaning seeped into the gaps between Angie's words, and into the silence that followed.

"I don't mind," Hannah said.

"Not even a little bit?"

"I don't know. Maybe. Sometimes. Doesn't have to be a big deal if we just tried it, right?"

"No, it doesn't," Angie said softly. Her eyes fluttered shut as they shifted closer to one another. They lay stiffly with their closed mouths pressed together, and then Angie's lips came alive.

When Angie moved on top of her, Hannah threw her arms around Angie's neck.

This was nothing like the time she and Oliver had kissed. This kiss didn't feel like pretending or waiting for it to finish. This made lights pop behind her eyes and made her stomach flip over. Angie's tongue in her mouth was soft and sweet. She didn't want it ever to end.

Hannah closed her eyes and kissed her back.

CHAPTER SIX

In the morning, when she rolled over toward the mattress on the floor next to her bed, Angie wasn't there. By the time she returned from the bathroom already showered and dressed, Viv was calling them for breakfast.

Viv spooned fluffy scrambled eggs onto the toast on their plates. Sometimes it felt like eggs were all Hannah ate when she was training, and she got sick of them, but she needed the protein.

Mark and Ethan took turns punching one another in the arm, wincing dramatically when they were hit.

"Would you stop it, you two? We have a guest!" Viv said.

"Angie doesn't mind. We're demonstrating boxing kangaroos for her, see?" Mark said, raising a fist toward Ethan again.

Hannah tried to catch Angie's eye, but Angie kept her eyes trained on her plate. While the twins showed off, she laughed politely but didn't say a word. After breakfast, Paul drove them to the pool, ranting the whole time about the football game he'd watched the day before.

Hannah and Angie swam for an hour and a half, the work unbroken by their usual games. When they were done, they moved on to the nearby gym to run on the treadmills.

She watched Angie's white and purple sneakers as her feet hit the ground. Their eyes met in the mirrored wall in front of them. She pushed hair, dampened from sweat, back from her face.

"You should get one of these," Angie said, pointing to her pink headband.

"No way. Lame!"

"Ha! You wish you could look this cool."

Did Hannah imagine it or did Angie's smile seem forced? Did she regret last night? It was terrifying to think that the way she kissed might be off-putting, that Angie could think of her in the same way Hannah thought about Oliver.

But that night, Angie crawled into her bed as soon as the lights were out. Before she flipped the switch, Angie put on a Talking Heads cassette. While the tape spooled one song into the next, they came together. They didn't speak, Angie's hands in her hair in the dark while they rolled around discovering. They fell asleep together, and Hannah woke up at dawn to the sound of Angie climbing back onto her mattress.

In the daytime, they kept their routine of getting up early to go to the pool. Though Hannah was tired from the late nights, her movements were fluid and strong. She swam length after length with Angie parallel to her, always just by her side or right behind her.

Without Tim pushing her, she was free to remember why she liked swimming in the first place. She pulled herself easily through the water, vowing that she'd try to hold onto this feeling somehow when Angie was gone.

There was only one week left for them to be together. Maybe something would happen. Angie's dad might need to continue working in Melbourne for a few extra days, or there might be a flight cancellation. Any delay in Angie leaving her would be better than nothing. Time counted down on a big red clock in her head, like a bomb was going to detonate.

At the pool's end, she paused. Angie finished her turn before she realized that Hannah had stopped. After a few moments, Angie swam back to her, treading water. She slid her goggles back, a deep impression from them around her eyes. Hannah pushed hers back too.

"Sorry, I just needed a minute," Hannah said.

"That's cool. Are you okay?"

"Yeah. Are you?"

Angie stared at her, then grinned. "I'm great."

"Good. I can't wait for you to meet my friends tonight."

"Me neither. They sound like fun. I want to see these chicks who are lucky enough to spend so much time with you. And I'm so excited about eating pizza," Angie's eyes rolled up toward the ceiling.

Hannah took Angie's hands under the water. They floated, their arms moving in circles together, legs kicking beneath them. Angie looked around, and when it was clear that the kids gathered in the shallow end weren't watching, she reached over the lane divider and hugged Hannah. Hannah clutched her shoulders, Angie's slight frame warm against hers in the water.

Paul drove them to Marie's place in the early evening. They climbed from the backseat of the wagon onto Marie's pebbled driveway. Statues of white stone were scattered on the lawn—angels, gargoyles, birds, and lions. Inside the two-story house was splashed with the color of feature walls and art prints.

As a kid, Hannah loved playing at Marie's house because of the bright decorations, and now she loved coming over because of the freedom. The place was so big that Marie and her sister had a rumpus room for themselves downstairs, with a bathroom and kitchenette.

Hannah pressed the doorbell, which played a loud electronic tune. Angie giggled, leaning against her and grabbing her shoulder. "I see what you mean. This place is so kitschy. I love it."

Marie answered the door with her hand on her hip. Her hair was swept to the side in a ponytail held in place by a scrunchie. "Hello."

"Hey. This is Marie, Marie this is Angie," Hannah said.

"Nice to meet you," Angie said.

Debbie was already there, so the introductions continued in the rumpus room. Like Marie, Debbie had curly hair but she achieved hers with a perm. When Debbie looked Angie up and down, Hannah was sure Debbie was comparing herself. She was sensitive about her upturned nose and freckles, no matter what anyone said to compliment her.

"I love your sweater!" Angie said to Debbie.

Hannah looked at the large geometric shapes in bright colors. She would never wear anything like that, but she could imagine Angie in it. Angie had so much more in common with her friends. It was easy to imagine Angie taking her place if she lived here, only she would never do anything like that.

They settled onto beanbags on the rust-brown carpet, and Marie's mother bustled in carrying a tray of sodas. Hannah had admitted to herself a couple of years ago that she had a crush on Mrs. Stevens. She was younger than the parents of most of her friends and always looked nice. Right now, there was a string of silver bracelets down her arm as she elegantly carried the tray, straight-backed and smiling.

"Girls, Mr. Stevens is picking up the pizzas right now and he'll be back any minute."

"Thank you, Mrs. Stevens," they chorused.

"So. What's been going on at school?" Hannah asked, reclining onto the beanbag with her cherry soda.

"You haven't missed anything. Except that Marie and Scott are over," Debbie replied.

"Oh no, are you okay?" Hannah asked. She didn't like Scott, but he was part of the popular group at school. Marie had been thrilled when he started paying attention to her, inviting her to parties at his house and sitting next to her in class.

"I'm fine. It was my idea. Scott's a moron. All boys are morons, I've decided," Marie said, examining her fingernails. "Who needs them, anyway?"

Hannah checked out Angie's reaction and quickly looked away. Angie was trying not to laugh, and she always wanted to laugh when Angie did. "Well, I'm sorry anyway."

"What about you, Angie? Are you dating anyone back home? I bet American boys are cute," Debbie said.

"No, not right now," Angie said, a flush creeping up her neck.

Mrs. Stevens came in with the pizza boxes, a roll of garlic bread placed on top of the stack. "Here we go, my darlings. We made sure we got a plain cheese one for you, Hannah."

"Thank you," she said.

She chewed on a slice, listening while her friends questioned Angie about what it was like to live in America. They talked about the food and the long summer vacation, and Marie asked if people dressed differently over there. Was it like they made it look on the movies? Marie was obsessed with Molly Ringwald and Angie had seen all her films too.

"I love the way you do your makeup, Angie," Debbie said, waving her finger at Hannah. "You should teach her how to do eyeliner like yours. It would look so good on her. I'm always trying to tell her."

Angie wiped grease from her chin with a napkin. "But Hannah's a natural beauty. She doesn't need it."

"Oh no, of course, she doesn't *need* it. I just think it would look good on her."

Marie tossed a balled-up napkin that hit Debbie in the face. "She's right, Debs. You're being a peer pressurer. Just say no, Hannah!"

Debbie froze then grabbed a discarded pizza crust to throw at Marie. They shrieked and Marie and Hannah pinned Debbie to the bottom of a pile of bodies. Hannah could make out Angie's muffled giggling as she joined the fray.

* * *

The day before Angie flew out, Angie lay down on her mattress as soon as they arrived home from training. Pulling the striped duvet over herself, she yawned, her hair fanning across the pillow.

"Don't let me sleep too long, okay?" she said. "Twenty minutes. It's my last day. I don't want to miss it."

"Okay, I won't," Hannah said.

"I just want to be able to stay up late with you tonight, okay?"

"It's all right. Don't worry. I'll wake you," Hannah said, but Angie was already gone.

She checked her watch then lay on her side, resting her chin on her forearm. When she was asleep Angie threw an elbow over her face, but she could still see her mouth, and the way her soft pink lips were slightly parted.

When the time had passed, Hannah said her name softly. Angie's eyes snapped open. They stared back at Hannah unfocused; then she pressed the heels of her palms into her eyes.

"Ugh, now I feel sad. I always feel sad when I wake up during the day like this. I shouldn't have gone to sleep."

"Come up here. It's okay. My parents won't come in when the door's closed," she said, taking Angie in her arms.

They kissed for a long time until Angie pulled away, sighing. Hannah lay on her back while Angie rested on her chest, clutching her shirt in a fist. Something about their pose made Hannah feel strong, grown up in a way she hadn't ever known.

"I can't believe I have to go home tomorrow. I hate it. I feel like shit," Angie said.

"I wish you didn't have to go too. I really do."

"You know...I..."

It was quiet. Hannah turned her head, brushing her lips against the top of Angie's head. "Angie? What do you want to say?"

"You know I like you for real, don't you? I'm not just pretending with you or anything dumb like that."

Hannah closed her eyes. How much could she say? How much should she risk? "I guess I was hoping so."

It was quiet again, then Angie pulled on her shirt. "You're such a dummy!"

"What do you mean? Why am I a dummy?"

"Well, do you like me back, or what?" Angie said, lifting Hannah's shirt. She pressed a crescent into her stomach with a fingernail once, and then again.

"Of course, I do! I like you a lot," Hannah said, drawing back enough for them to kiss. "Like, really like you."

"You do?"

"I do. I've been thinking that I wanted to ask you something. You can say no if you want. I know you live so far away, and we won't get to see each other much. But…would you…want to be my girlfriend?"

Until now, as much as she'd been thinking about it, she couldn't say it aloud. She worried that this was only practice for Angie. The magazines Marie read had articles about this stuff, and they said that girls who had crushes on other girls usually grew out of it.

Hannah didn't think she would grow out of it, and since meeting Angie, she didn't want to.

"Of course, I do! It doesn't matter about the distance. We can still write letters to each other all the time," Angie said with a smile in her voice.

"The distance doesn't bother you?"

"Well, yeah, of course, I wish we lived in the same place. But I don't like anyone at home. I only like you."

"Me neither. I'll send you mixtapes and cards. I want to give you something now," Hannah said, staring around the room. If only she had a ring or a bracelet. She knew how much Angie liked her watch, so she pulled the band out from one of its loops. "Here. You can have the mermaids."

"I can't take your watch!" Angie said, wide-eyed.

"I want you to have it."

Hannah helped her put it on, Angie adjusting it so the face pointed inward.

"Thank you. I'll treasure it. I really will," Angie said, kissing her cheek. "I'm so glad I met you, Hannah."

"Me too."

Her girlfriend. Hannah couldn't believe it.

CHAPTER SEVEN

2000 - Melbourne

Hannah tipped shredded wheat into a bowl, garnishing it with a sliced banana. Before sitting down to eat, she dashed across the room gathering plates and mugs to dump in the sink. A basket of clothes she'd taken from the line the day before sat on the kitchen table. Hannah roughly folded shirts and underwear and then ran the basket to her room.

Aside from her car, Hannah's two-bedroom townhouse was the only purchase she had to show for her swimming career. It was usually immaculate, but with being so busy lately, she'd let things slide. Marie was coming over tonight, but Hannah wanted it to look good for herself too.

The apartment was especially lovely in the morning. Sun streamed in from the sliding glass door at the rear, casting buttery light over the polished hardwood floor. Framed black-and-white photos of her family lined the stairwell, and she'd invested in a few pieces of antique furniture. She was spending less time here lately, but it was her sanctuary and her favorite place in the world.

Powering up the computer in her study nook, she shoveled cereal into her mouth, waiting for the screen to light up. This time was precious, moments snatched from the jaws of her team. She was due at the gym in an hour to see her trainer, then she would go back to the pool to swim under Neil's supervision, and after that, there was a massage booked.

It was two weeks since she'd seen Angie. Why did Angie ask if it was okay to email if she wasn't planning to follow through? She hated how compulsively she'd been checking. She promised herself that she'd only look once this morning.

She put her hand on her throat. A bold unread email waited for her.

Hey Hannah,

Sorry it's taken me a while to write. I've been thinking about it a lot, and I wanted to wait until I knew what I wanted to say.

Again, congratulations on the trial. You killed it out there, and I loved watching that race. I have every confidence in you, I really do. I think you're more powerful than you've ever been, surer of yourself in the water in a way that can only come from experience. Not blind faith like we had back then when we were younger and didn't know what we were getting ourselves into! And I'm not just saying this because I'm on the coaching team and I want you to make us look good! I know you will anyway.

So, to what I've been wanting to say. I didn't know how to bring it up when I saw you, and I came to your place in Bondi that day with every intention of saying it, but I didn't know quite how to handle things. I don't know how to act, and I get the feeling that you don't either.

What I wanted to say to you was that I've always felt bad about the way things went down between us. I wonder if you've spent as much time thinking about it as I have. Probably not.

I want to be able to talk about this stuff with you, because for a while you were my best friend. I know friends come and go in life, but in these past years, I don't think I've ever felt as close to anyone as I did with you. And when I saw you, it was like I was a teenager again, remembering all this stuff and how close we were, how we could talk about everything. Being friends with you made me feel so much less alone.

You were kinder to me than I deserved, but I could tell you were still angry with me or wary of me or whatever, and I don't blame you one bit. But thanks for talking to me anyway. You don't know how much it means.

Anyway, I just wanted to bring it up, so we could talk about it and clear the air.

Does any of this make sense to you at all?

- A.

Hannah shoved the mouse away as though it might bite her. What was she supposed to say to that? Taking a deep breath, she positioned her fingers on the keyboard.

A moment later she changed her mind again. No, Angie could wait, like she'd waited all these years.

That night Marie burst into Hannah's place, carrying a foil-wrapped tray and a six-pack of beer. She kicked the door behind her, blowing a lock of hair from her face. Hannah chuckled at the sight of her best friend using her ass to press the door back into place. She always left the door unlocked for Marie, who was never great with knocking anyway.

"Hey, hey! Cheat night is here. I'm here for you! Nachos and beer, has there ever been a better marriage?"

"What about your marriage?"

"Don't even talk about Scott. He's in my bad books right now," Marie said, setting the tray and beer down. She opened the drawer under the counter, cutlery rattling around until her hand reappeared with a bottle opener. "He's such a shit. Came home so late after his big night out with the boys."

"Oh no, not coming home late!" she said. "How will your marriage ever survive?"

Marie flipped open the beers. "You can make fun as much as you want, but he kept me awake for hours! Mumbling and singing songs from whatever trashy sports bar they were hanging out in. I made sure I got up extra early and banged around in the kitchen."

Marie walked over with the drinks, cackling. Hannah took plates from the cupboard and laid them on the table, adding a roll of paper towel to the center.

"You're such a harpy," she said.

"I tell you, you have the right idea, being single," Marie said, dropping a pile of nachos onto her plate.

"It's not a choice at this point. How would I even have time for a girlfriend with the way my schedule is?"

"You'd make time if you truly wanted one."

They ate in happy silence, Hannah licking sour cream from her fingers. She'd been craving junk food for days.

"I'm going to eat so much crap when this is all done. Once in a blue moon is not enough," she said. She jogged her leg, glancing over her shoulder toward her study nook.

The monitor's green light blinked. She didn't have the heart to turn it all the way off; the computer only slept.

"Am I keeping you from something? Are you watching porn to keep you warm at night? It's so much easier to get with the net," Marie said.

"Not my thing. It's nothing. I owe someone an email. That's all."

Marie raised her eyebrows. "Someone? Is that what you're calling her these days?"

There was a brief standoff in which Hannah pulled a chip from the pile, and Marie raised her eyebrows even higher.

"Okay yes, you're right. It's Angie. She finally got in touch. I don't know what to say to her now, though. There was all this stuff about how we were best friends," she said, using air quotes.

"Well, that's just stupid. Angie wasn't your best friend, I was."

"Yeah. You're kind of missing the point."

"I'm kidding! I'm sorry, Hannah. That must have been weird. That is an odd thing for her to say," Marie said, tipping her head back to collect the last drop from her beer bottle.

She shrugged. "I feel like she's trying to apologize and yet…not? Like, sorry it happened, but it was not at all a proper apology the more I think about it. Do you know what I mean?"

"I think I know exactly what you mean. Scott is a master of the non-apology. He's always saying he's sorry that I'm upset as if he has nothing to do with it. As if it's not his dickish behavior that makes me mad in the first place! Have you replied to her yet?"

"No. I don't know what to say. Not the faintest idea. I should say something, though, right? It feels mean to just say nothing. Don't you think?"

"I guess so. At least you're telling me about it this time and not clamming up like you used to do! Can't believe I didn't even know you were gay back then. Hey, do you know if she has a boyfriend yet?"

"I don't know anything about her. I know she's separated from Mr. Golden Boy because they mentioned it when I saw her on TV. But that's all I know."

"Haven't you tried to find out online? I mean, isn't that the best thing about her being famous like you are? You can just look it up."

"No, I haven't. I don't want to be a creep."

Looking at images on the Internet was one thing, but she planned to stay away from trying to learn Angie's relationship status. She'd found out about her ex by accident and she didn't need to know more. Hannah certainly didn't want Marie to find out that she'd been looking at Angie's photos.

"Okay, suit yourself. But I would if I were you," Marie said. She chewed, staring off into space.

Hannah leaned over and flicked Marie's forehead. "What are you thinking about?"

"Nothing. It's just if you think about it, Scott was a jerk when we were teenagers, and I know I complain about him now, but of course, he's a good guy. Maybe she's not so bad? People can change a lot when they're growing up. Maybe she doesn't know what to say?"

Hannah shrugged. "Maybe."

They finished the nachos, then spread out on the sofa to watch a double episode of *Law and Order*. Marie chattered loudly throughout, identifying red herrings and the actual murderer as soon as she saw him. It was annoying, but at least it meant Hannah could be distracted from composing an email in her head.

After Scott picked up Marie, Hannah wiped down the table and took the empty beer bottles out to recycle. While she washed and dried her hands, she tried to convince herself to go to bed.

She stood in front of the computer for a moment, then pressed the space bar to wake it up. If she didn't reply now, she'd think about it all night.

There was another email from Angie.

Hey, sorry if I upset you before. I mean, maybe you haven't read it yet but sorry anyway. I know you're busy. I don't mean to be annoying. Just forget I said anything if you think that's best.

She balled up her hands then stretched her fingers out over the keyboard. It was kind of shitty to make Angie wait all day for a reply.

Hey Angie,

It's okay. Just needed time to think today. I don't know if angry is the right word for it. It's kind of weird seeing one another again after all this time.

You're right. I don't know how to act. I'm not quite sure what to say either. We were so young. When I looked at Rachel Willis at the trials, I realized she was about the same age as we were back then. And not to patronize her, but she's a baby! It would be silly of me to hold any of what happened against you. I'm sure we've both changed a lot.

I'm happy to start over with a clean slate if you are. I don't like the thought of you feeling bad over things that are so far back in the past.

I'm happy to chat with you again and get to know one another as adults. We're going to see one another around anyway, and I don't want it to be unpleasant.

Hannah

She hit the send button before she could obsess over what she'd written. There was no reason to think anymore about it. It was a lifetime ago, and they were different people now.

She had to stop holding on to the past if she ever wanted to move forward.

CHAPTER EIGHT

1987 - Melbourne

Hannah seized the phone on the first ring before anyone else could. The whole family knew she was expecting to hear from Angie for her birthday, and she couldn't take any chances. Ethan and Mark loved intercepting her calls on the extension near the living room.

Getting a private line in her bedroom had taken extensive lobbying. Paul and Viv were fanatical about not letting her chip into her earnings. They deposited every cent into an account that she could only touch on her twenty-first birthday.

She vacuumed, swept and mopped to earn her hamburger-shaped phone. It was just like one she'd seen on TV, the numbers set on a slice of yellow cheese. When she opened the bun and put it to her ear, two beeps confirmed it was a long-distance call. She was beaming before she heard Angie's voice.

"Happy birthday, sweet sixteen!"

"Thanks!"

"Tell me all about what you're doing today. I want to hear all about it. I wish I were there with you so bad. I miss you so much, on special days more than ever. What kind of cake are you having?"

"I'm hanging out with Debbie and Marie tonight, and I asked Viv if I could have an ice-cream cake."

"Sounds fun. Will you say hi to Debbie and Marie for me? Did you get the package I sent you?"

"I did, thank you so much! I love the bracelet."

"You do? I know you don't wear much jewelry, but I thought you'd like it. I knew it would suit you."

"Of course, I do," Hannah said, raising her wrist over her face to look at it again. The small blue stone centered on a thin band was just right for her. "I love silver. I'll wear it every day. I should have said that first, sorry. Why do I get all tongue-tied on these calls?"

"Because we never get to talk? I've been nervous all day about calling! Nervous all week, but a good kind of nervous. So, don't worry about anything. I'm just glad you like the bracelet. I like thinking about you wearing it. I always wear your watch. I'm looking at it right now! Are you sure the bracelet is okay? Because if you didn't like it, I'd want to get you something else. Don't worry about hurting my feelings. It's more important to me that you like it."

"I really, really like it. I promise."

"I'm glad. I loved picking it out. So…How are you doing with training? Not so long until the trials for Seoul. I'm so nervous about it. Freaking. Out. Are you nervous?"

"Kind of. Tim's happy with how I'm doing, for once," Hannah said, her mouth twisting around her coach's name.

The day before they'd been working on the angle of her hands as they hit the water, and she was proud of how well she'd taken his feedback. But when he complimented her, it sounded sarcastic, like he was insulting her for not getting it right sooner.

"So, you think you'll definitely make it in then? Like, your times are that good?"

"I don't know. Probably."

Everyone seemed to think so. The *Sunday Courier* last weekend had a front-page photo spread with Hannah's face in the middle, sandwiched between other Australian swimmers. When she saw a copy of it on the kitchen counter, she flipped it over.

It was weird to walk through the supermarket with her mother now too. On their way to the checkout, they passed racks of women's magazines with her face plastered across the covers.

She spiraled the phone cord around her finger, wondering if she should talk to Angie about how she was feeling. A few nights ago, she rose to get a glass of water and paused outside of the kitchen. Paul often had a glass of scotch before bed, to wind down when he was working the late shift. Her mother was out there too.

Hannah heard her name and hovered, gathering up pieces of the conversation.

"I don't know; I feel like they're starting to sexualize her. She's not even sixteen yet! Did you see how much makeup they put on her at that photo shoot? She's a swimmer, not a fashion model. I don't want her to start getting self-conscious. She's already always hunching because of her height. And she's not the kind of kid who even enjoys it, not that I wouldn't still be worried if she did. Do you know what I mean?"

It was easier to hear Paul's deep voice. "I don't think we have to worry too much about her, honey. We can't control what the world does, but she's such a sensible kid. It's normal for girls her age to get a bit worried about their bodies. Isn't it?"

When Viv answered, her voice was quieter, and Hannah couldn't make it out. She went back to her room without her drink, her mouth dry.

It was silent on the other end of the line, and she realized that she hadn't spoken for a while. "What about you, how are you tracking with getting there?"

"Well, I have to get there! Not going is just not an option."

"Remember how we talked about how putting too much pressure on yourself is bad? It's okay if you don't win," she said gently.

Before, she'd envied Angie for her parents, who poured everything into Angie's swimming career. Angie's mother was practically her full-time driver, ferrying Angie to her training sessions and staying to cheer her on. It took time for Hannah to understand that the support came with a hefty price tag.

"I'm not putting pressure on myself to *win*! It's not that at all. If I don't get there. I don't get to see you. That's what I really care about."

"Oh."

Hannah looked toward her door, raising the phone closer to her mouth. "I want to see you too. I love your letters, but…"

"I know. It's not the same. I keep thinking, one day when we're older, imagine if we lived in the same place? How awesome would that be? Whether you moved over here to Austin, or I moved over there…I don't care which way it is. Maybe we could even do both someday, like, go back and forth together. Don't you think that would be awesome?"

"It would be. It would be really, super awesome."

They each fell quiet, and she stared at the collage on her wall. There were photos of the two of them from that night after Luna Park, arm-in-arm. Taped up next to them were press clippings Angie had cut from magazines to send to her. Bordering the photos were pictures from magazines of Rob Lowe and Emilio Estevez. Hannah put them there to throw her brothers off the scent.

She listened to Angie's breathing, picturing a cord traveling for miles and miles under the ocean to link them together.

If she could swim there, she would.

On the morning of the trials for the Olympics, Hannah stood in her room, bouncing on the balls of her feet.

She had prepared as well as she could for this day, and now there was nothing she could do but swim. She kissed her palm and pressed it to Angie's face.

Even at the World Championships, she had never seen anything like the size of this crowd. When she turned to wave at the audience, she gained strength from the fact that her parents were there with Mark and Ethan.

The swimming federation gave her tickets to invite as many people as she wanted, so Marie and Debbie were here too. It was a school day; they were almost as excited to have the day off as they were to see her swim.

There were a lot of reasons to win, and Angie was the most important one. She could imagine her standing close to her block, encouraging her like she did when they were training. They were in this together now.

This race would be dedicated to her. To her girlfriend.

Hannah exploded into the water, unstoppable.

That night she sat down at her desk. It was too late in Austin to call Angie now, but she wanted to run a letter down to the post box as soon as she could. Angie would check the news to find out if Hannah qualified, but it wasn't a sure thing for the American media to feature Australian swimmers.

I've made it! I mean, I hope I get into more events and I'll write to you again to let you know if I have. But now I know that it's really happening for sure. I can't believe it! A thousand times good luck with yours next week. Let's make sure that we get the chance to talk on the phone again when you qualify. That's right, I said WHEN because I know that you will.

* * *

A couple of weeks later Hannah and Angie compared notes on the phone. They talked about their post-trial press conferences and swapped borrowed stories about the Olympics from teammates who'd already been there.

The two of them had qualified for the two hundred- and four hundred-meter freestyle events. Hannah was also going to be part of the team for the two hundred-meter freestyle relay.

"I heard the Olympic village is amazing! The food is going to be so good. Let's make sure we get to spend every meal together. I don't care if I don't get to spend any time with my team at all, if you want to know the truth. I just want to hang out with you," Angie said.

"Me too. Hey, thanks again for the mixtape you sent me. I listen to it like, all the time."

"You do? I was worried you wouldn't like it. I know my taste isn't as cool as yours."

"Don't be silly! I love it."

"Good. 'Cos I'm working on another one for you right now. I've been taping songs off the radio, every time I get the chance. Hey listen, I should wrap it up. But I'll write you another letter tomorrow, okay? I promise."

"You got it. Miss you," Hannah said. She held the receiver long after the click sounded.

* * *

Hannah's training regime intensified as the Olympics approached. Tim pushed her further than ever before, pacing up and down the side of the pool with his stopwatch in hand. In his early thirties now, he'd once been a champion swimmer, known for being stubborn in the pool. He was heavy for a swimmer, but he'd never let it slow him down.

She struggled to recall what he looked like when he smiled; it was so rare. He frowned down at his stopwatch while his lips worked soundlessly. She preferred that he spoke to himself if it meant he left her alone for a while.

Still, she had to admit that with his help, her times were good. He'd instructed her to swim slow laps while they worked on tightening up her stroke, and now he was finally letting her swim at a natural pace. For four hours each day, she was in the pool, barely leaving enough time to keep up with her homework and write to Angie.

The schedule was so crazy that it was a couple of days before she noticed that the letter Angie promised her hadn't come. Angie wrote like she talked and sent multi-page letters no matter what was going on. Sometimes she wrote under the covers, holding a flashlight over the page.

The weekend arrived, and Hannah still hadn't heard anything. It wasn't like Angie, but she must be confused. She must have forgotten that it was her turn.

Dear Angie,

How are you? You forgot my letter! But I'll forgive you, haha. I bet you're so busy. I am too. Training has been crazy. All I dream about is swimming, going back and forth in the pool all day long. Sometimes you visit me in my dreams, though, so that's nice. Thanks for stopping by.

Things are okay at school. Home has been a bit of a war zone. Mark got into a fight at school, punched some guy and got sent to H7. That's where they send the naughty kids, and he's the first one in our family to get sent there. So Viv and Paul were both really mad. He got grounded and now Ethan won't stop complaining because they usually go out together so much.

Have you been watching that show Full House*? I think it's a bit cheesy, but Paul thinks it's hilarious.*

Love, Hannah xo

Another two weeks passed. It could take a while for the post to arrive all the way from America, but to get nothing by now was scary. It was a hole in the pit of Hannah's stomach, keeping her awake at night and robbing her of focus in the water.

On Friday afternoon, Viv picked her up from practice. Hannah looked hopefully at Viv, still leaning across the seat, opening the door to let her in with her armload of gear.

"I'm sorry honey, nothing came today."

She got into the car and pulled the door shut heavily, leaning her elbow against the window. Now the mail wouldn't come again until Monday. What if Angie was hurt or sick? She had told her folks Angie was her best friend, but she wasn't sure what Angie told her parents. There was no way of knowing if Hannah was significant enough to be notified if something went wrong.

Viv lightly touched her hair. Still staring out the window, she brushed it away.

"Hannah…"

"I don't want to talk about it."

"I know you two are close, but she's training just like you are."

"She was always training! But she found time before."

"Darling, she's all the way over in another country. You don't know what's going on. It could be anything. It might have gotten lost in the post, or she's busy, or she…I don't know, got a boyfriend or something. Or got a new best friend. I hate to say it Hannah, but girls your age are not always the most reliable people."

"You don't get it! Something's wrong," she said, fighting tears.

"Hannah, if you're going to be this worried…You're under a lot of stress right now. If there's something you can do to make it better, do it. Call her."

"I thought I might. This weekend. It'll be okay to call in the morning, I'll try to call her then."

"Okay. I think that's a good idea."

The plan made her feel a little better. She put her arm outside, waving it in the air, hoping she could make this dread disappear in the morning.

CHAPTER NINE

2000 - Melbourne

Hannah pushed her shoulders back, forcing herself out of her natural slouch. The building extended as far into the sky as she could see from down here, the mirrored windows reflecting the city onto itself.

Somewhere inside this skyscraper, there was a photographer and a journalist waiting to drain her like the vampires they were. Throughout her career, Hannah had met decent writers who cared about their craft, but none of them published in *Ladies Weekly*.

The fact that Angie was going to be there added to her nerves. They hadn't emailed one another again, and their last exchange hadn't done much to clear the air.

After pushing through the revolving door, she walked up to a counter by the entrance. A receptionist with platinum blond hair barely looked at her, pointing toward the elevator using the hand that wasn't holding the phone.

In the mirror lining the wall, she checked out her face, which was free of makeup. The black jeans and white V-neck shirt were fine, but she'd feel bad about herself soon enough when they changed everything about the way she looked.

She came to a door with the magazine's title inscribed in large gold letters. *Ladies Weekly* was the type of magazine Viv read and bitched about before passing it onto friends. It was packed with articles about Australian celebrities and the royal family.

Hannah's manager Eric had pressed her to do this interview. As always, the goal was to shape a storyline about her, one that would make the public love her. It had the trickle-down effect of helping to secure endorsement deals. Besides, this piece wasn't just about her. It was about the team. Didn't she want to be a team player?

She introduced herself to another receptionist, a guy behind a glass-topped desk. A name tag said his name was Marcus.

"Oh great, you're here. I think they've been waiting for you. I'll buzz them. Yes, hello. Ms. Clark is here."

Marcus peered at her, his eyes kind behind heavy-framed glasses. "I have to tell you, I'm a geek for swimming, and I'm such a big fan of yours. I hope you take home some gold."

"Thank you so much," Hannah replied. It was always obvious when the well wishes of strangers were genuine.

A woman's heels clicked across the marble floor as she came toward them. Her rail-thin figure made Hannah wonder if she moonlighted as a model.

"Hi there, I'm Dominique. I'll be taking care of you today. Please come with me."

Dominique escorted her to a room with a bare cement floor and high ceiling. The warehouse-like space had the feel of wanting to imitate somewhere hipper and more real. People clustered around lights on stands, and the black umbrellas to shade them. Some of the members of the chattering group stopped to look at her as she passed by with Dominique.

When they entered the next room, Hannah stopped before walking forward. Angie sat with her eyes closed. A purple-haired makeup artist applied smoky color to Angie's eyelid, only glancing over when Hannah spoke.

"Oh. Hey," Hannah said, sliding into a black vinyl chair.

"Hannah? Is that you?" Angie asked.

"Yep, it's me."

"How are you? I don't know if you've heard, but it's just going to be the two of us now. I only found out when I got here, or I would have called your manager to make sure he knew. You know how it is. They change these things all the time. Working on a different angle or whatnot. They're doing a story about washed-up old me and the hot favorite to take out the two hundred meters."

She gripped the armrests of her chair. Another makeup artist with dreadlocks stood behind her, her willowy figure draped in a flowing black dress.

"What do you mean? I thought Rachel and a few of the other girls were going to be here?"

"Hey, Hannah. I'm Rachelle. I'm going to be working on you today. I've been given instructions by the stylist, but is there anything you want to tell me before I start?"

"Huh? Oh no. I don't care. Angie, when did all this happen?"

Her brow furrowed as she met Hannah's gaze in the mirror. Her eyes stood out under the heavy makeup. "I don't know. They just told me when I got here like I told you. I honestly had nothing to do with it. Do you not want to do this? We can talk to them if you want, I'll back you up on it if it's that important to you to decline, we can…"

Hannah eyed one makeup artist and then the other. Each of them fiddled with their tools, pretending they weren't listening. "No, of course not. It's fine."

Rachelle used a finger to tilt Hannah's face toward her, and she gritted her teeth.

After their faces were painted and their hair was done, Dominique took them into yet another room, gesturing to the red chaise lounge. It was the only piece of furniture save for the black armchair across from it, and a coffee table with three plastic water bottles on the surface.

"The interview will happen in here, and then I'll take you to wardrobe to pick out some clothes before the shoot happens. Can I get either of you anything? Coffee?" Dominique asked.

"No thank you," Angie and Hannah replied together.

Dominique exited, leaving them alone. The silence lengthened while Hannah grabbed a water bottle and unscrewed the lid.

Angie leaned toward her. "Bet you didn't miss all of this, huh?"

"You'd win that bet. They made me look like a painted clown," she said. When she wore makeup at all, she preferred a natural look. As Rachelle layered colors on her, she'd watched herself disappear.

"I always said you didn't need makeup. Still, I think you look gorgeous," Angie said, from close beside her on the lounge.

"You don't have to say that, but thanks."

"I mean it," Angie replied, her green-eyed stare dropping to Hannah's lips.

"You look…nice too," Hannah said, cutting her eyes away from Angie's bow-shaped mouth and high cheekbones.

Hannah had almost called her beautiful.

The journalist strode in, her slick black hair cut into a bob with bangs, her lips rimmed with bright red lipstick. The determination on her face made Hannah sure that she was going to be hard work.

"Hello ladies," she said, shaking each of their hands. "I'm Veronica. It's lovely to meet you both."

On the edge of the black armchair, Veronica crossed her legs before resting a black dictation machine on the coffee table. With a long finger, Veronica showily pressed the button to record.

The questions were predictable, following the comeback template. At first, the interrogation focused solely on Hannah. Can you describe your training regime? Your diet? How do you balance your personal and professional lives? Do you think you're going to add a gold medal to your achievements? Take me through the decision-making process that led to your return to swimming?

Though the questions were boring, it was easy to give canned answers while Angie sat quietly beside her. It wasn't as embarrassing as Hannah had feared, and at least Angie might be able to see that she'd developed more confidence with this stuff.

"Given your status as former rivals in the pool, how do the two of you get along now?" Veronica asked.

Hannah and Angie looked at one another for a beat. It was intended to throw them off balance and she wasn't going to bite. She crossed her arms, and Angie cleared her throat.

"I have only respect for Hannah. She's a fantastic swimmer, and though we haven't started working together much yet, it will be an honor when we do."

"I agree," Hannah replied.

"It's certainly a strange situation, to have you in this role, Angie. An American assisting with coaching the Aussies. There has always been such a fierce professional rivalry between the two countries," Veronica said.

"I'm sorry, is there a question in there somewhere?" Hannah asked.

Her faux-syrupy tone mirrored Veronica's, making Angie burst into giggles beside her. Veronica's face turned to stone.

"Well, how has the professional rivalry impacted you now?"

"I think we just answered that, didn't we?" Angie replied.

Veronica's eyebrows flicked up. "Okay. Well, those are all the questions I have. I'll get Dom for you. She can take you to the wardrobe department."

Veronica shook hands with them again, more brusquely this time. Scooping up the recording device, she left without turning it off.

"Was there a question in there somewhere? That was too good," Angie said.

"Sorry, she asked me so many questions. I don't know why they bothered to ask us for a joint interview if she was going to do that. Guess we didn't give them the catfight they wanted."

When Hannah met Angie's eye, Angie gently squeezed her knee. "You don't have to apologize. It's not your fault. I'm happy to be here, anyway."

Hannah started to reply, but Dominique flung the door open. She crooked a beckoning finger. "Time to change. Come with me, please."

"Why does it always sound so ominous when they give directions?" Angie whispered, and Hannah smirked. "Hey, I've got an idea. Let's pick the most ridiculous outfits we can find in there. But we'll act as if we like them. It'll be fun. What do you think?"

"Hey, I'm in. Anything to make this even a tiny bit less horrible."

They checked out the outfits the stylist had put together, which were all dresses. Hannah screwed up her nose at the plunging necklines and metal accents. She would never wear this stuff, not even for a photo shoot.

Angie turned to the stylist, Max, and shook her head emphatically. He threw a hand up in the air.

"What's the problem?" Max asked.

"I'm sorry, but I don't think any of this stuff represents the right look for us. Can we see other choices please?" Angie asked sweetly.

"All right. You can go to wardrobe. Whatever."

Dominique guided Angie and Hannah to a room filled with clothing and headless mannequins. They rifled through racks of garments, whispering with their heads bent together.

"I can't believe they let us loose in here," Hannah said. "What do you think this is supposed to be? A dress or a shirt?" She held the sheer item against her chest, tilting her head to the side and vamping.

Angie covered her mouth. "I don't know, but it's awful! You have to pick that one."

"No way. I don't mind looking stupid, but that's way too short. Not to mention see-through. Oh my god, look at this! What is this supposed to be, a jumpsuit? A romper?"

"A pantsuit? A joined together pantsuit," Angie said, running her fingers over the fabric, which was dangerously close to being polyester.

Hannah touched the long line of buttons on the front of the suit. "I can't believe I'm going to do this, but this is the one for me."

"Perfect. Just perfect. It looks like it'll fit you just right too. What do you think about this for me?" Angie asked, holding up a blue dress with shoulder pads and a vinyl sash.

"I can't believe we're already throwing back to the eighties, but yes, I think you must."

They changed in adjoining dressing rooms, giggling behind the black curtains.

"I'm starting to have misgivings about this," Hannah said, biting her lip as she stared at herself in the floor-length mirror. The red and white suit made her look like a praying mantis, all broad shoulders and long limbs. "This is even more ridiculous than it looked on the hanger. I'll never live it down."

Angie threw the curtain open, her mouth hanging open as she looked Hannah up and down. "Oh my god! I can't believe it, but that looks kind of good on you. You're going to start a trend of weird jumpsuits!"

Hannah stepped toward Angie. "Hey, likewise. That color is lovely."

Angie placed her hand on her shoulder, looking up at her. They stood in silence, brown eyes looking into green.

"This is so much more fun with you, you know? It always was," Angie said. She smoothed her hands over Hannah's shoulders, then straightened the jumpsuit's collar.

Hannah's hands rested at her sides. They wanted to betray her, itching to curl around Angie's body. The sash accentuated her lovely hourglass shape.

They looked to the door at the sound of Max's voice. He was watching them, calculating the damage. After a moment, he clicked his fingers.

"Not what I would have chosen, but you don't look half bad. Come on. I'm going to introduce you to the photographer."

Hannah and Angie exchanged a knowing look when they met Zen, the long-haired photographer with a manicured goatee. Of course, his name was Zen. He surveyed each of them with his mouth downturned.

They mugged for the camera, Angie winking at Hannah as she sucked in her cheeks with an exaggerated smolder.

"Closer," Zen said in a monotone from behind the camera. "And closer again."

Hannah rolled her eyes, then pulled Angie toward her. They stood arm in arm, Angie's head resting in the crook of her neck, her honey-scented shampoo bringing a rush of sense memory. Was it possible that Angie still used the same shampoo all these years later?

Finally, Zen called an end to the shoot and Dominique shepherded them back to the wardrobe department to change. Hannah unbuttoned the jumpsuit, peeling it down her waist and wondering what Marie's face would look like when she saw the pictures. They'd be laughing about this for years.

"So, how long are you down here in Melbourne? Did you come down just for this fabulous media opportunity, or do you have other business?" Hannah asked.

"I'm here through the weekend, the work part is all done for now. I did have other meetings, but I'm done with all my commitments, which is nice. I don't fly back until Sunday, so I was planning to have a look around, see the sights a bit. This is such a beautiful country, so I'm trying to see as much of it as I can. I haven't been here since…not for a long time…"

Hannah stared at the wall that divided them. She could be an adult about this. As Angie said, it had been a long time, and they were getting along fine. Barely any weirdness at all today. "Do you have dinner plans? We can go somewhere. I mean, if you want to."

It took so long for Angie to answer that Hannah wondered if she'd heard. Then there was the sound of the curtain rings scraping along the rod as she exited her cubicle.

"I'd love that, Hannah. I really would."

CHAPTER TEN

Hannah leaned over to get closer to her reflection, widening her eyes and brushing mascara along her lashes. "Shit," she said when she stabbed the wand into her lid. She used a cotton ball to wipe the black smudge away.

On the basin's edge, Marie's voice blared from the cordless phone. "I can't believe you're going on a date with her. This is crazy. After all this time, you're still into her, and she's still into you. I know you hate it when I get into your business but should I be worried about you?"

Hannah glared at the phone, then lifted it to her mouth and pressed the button that switched it over from speaker. "Why would you think this is a date? That's not what I said. We're going out to dinner because she's in town. I'm just being nice."

When there was no answer, she shifted the phone to her other ear, frowning. "Hello? You still there?"

"Sure. Sorry, my bad. So, what are you wearing?"

She shrugged even though Marie couldn't see her. "Nothing fancy. Jeans and that sleeveless black top I got when we went shopping at McCullers. Remember?"

"I do. It's very nice on you. And where are you going?"

"She wants to see Lygon Street. I thought I'd take her to Francesco's."

"Okay, well, have a good night. Call me tomorrow and tell me how it went?"

"Sure."

She gripped the edges of the sink, looking at herself and taking a deep breath. She hadn't meant for the dinner suggestion to be read as a come-on. What if she'd given that impression to Angie too? Her reflection shook her head back at her, and together they agreed it was too late to back out now.

They'd agreed to meet on a Lygon Street corner, Melbourne's Little Italy. She walked the short block from her tram stop and watched Angie from a few paces back. She was finger-combing her hair, searching the street. Her black winter coat hung open so that Hannah could see the emerald-coloured dress underneath. Hannah didn't have to see her up close to know she looked gorgeous.

"Hey Angie," Hannah said as she walked up, her heart jumping at the look on Angie's face when Hannah appeared.

"Hey there. You look so lovely."

"Oh…thanks. So do you."

"Thanks. So, this seems nice. Where's good here?"

"There's a place just down the street that's my favorite."

They strode together past tables cluttering the street, where people drank red wine and ate their pasta on checked tablecloths.

A man in a white apron stood in front of the door to a restaurant they passed, holding out a menu toward them. "Hey beautiful ladies, you looking for dinner? You want to try the best gnocchi on the street?"

Hannah waved and shook her head. Angie looked back and asked, "What's the deal?"

"Oh, this is just how they roll along here. Everyone tries to get you to come into their place. Here we are."

"Hello! My favorite customer. How are you, Ms. Clark?"

Abdul had been working there for almost as long as Hannah had been coming, and she always enjoyed talking to him. His dark hair was tied back in a ponytail, a gold hoop in one ear.

"I'm well, thanks, Abdul. Can we get a table inside?"

"Of course, of course. And I'll instruct the chef to make your dinner extra special—we all like knowing that we're giving you fuel to race. You come here to carb load, right?" he asked, winking at her as he pulled out a chair. He did the same for Angie, then handed them red leather-bound menus.

"You know it," Hannah replied.

"This is lovely," Angie said, looking around at the warm brick walls, the dark green tablecloths that matched the heavy drapes. Between them, a white candle dripped wax onto the side of a wine bottle acting as a holder. Hannah watched the flame guttering for a moment. No wonder Marie had reacted the way she had when they talked earlier.

"Sorry if it looks kind of cheesy. A lot of places along here have candles and all that stuff," Hannah said. "The food's good though, I promise."

"I'm sure I'll like it," Angie said, picking up the menu eagerly. She scanned the list before closing it and waving her hand. "You know what? I'm happy for you to order for us. You already know this place, and I bet you know what all the best dishes are anyway. And I like everything; I'm not fussy at all. Can we share?"

"Oh, I..."

"I'm happy to eat vegetarian dishes. If you still don't eat meat, I mean..." Her hands clasped in front of her on the table, her back straight as she looked across at Hannah.

Abdul arrived to fill their water glasses, tilting the bottle toward them one after the other. "Can I get you lovely ladies something to drink?"

Angie looked expectantly at her. Hannah ordered them a bottle of wine, Angie nodding when she named a red.

When Abdul was gone Angie twisted her earring around, quickly looking away from her.

Angie's face was thinner, and there were subtle lines around her mouth. In the intervening years, Angie had only grown more beautiful, but buried under the woman's face were the features of the girl she had loved.

She caught the silly thought. That was not love. She'd only believed that when she was a teenager who had no way of knowing any better. Since Angie she'd been in two long-term relationships, one with a woman who trained at the same gym and another with a woman Marie had introduced her too. Both relationships had showed her what love was, even if in some ways it had always felt like something was missing. She was slow to trust, and couldn't help blaming Angie for that sometimes.

"You okay?" Angie said softly.

"Of course," she said, wiping her palms on her jeans. "So okay, I'll order us a pizza and pasta to share. What do you think?"

"Sounds great to me."

Abdul was back a moment later, taking their order and removing their menus with an assurance that they'd ordered well—the best items in the house, as far as he was concerned.

Angie sat up straighter, and she took a deep breath. "How are your folks doing? Viv and Paul? Such nice people. And your brothers? How are they?"

"They're good. Mark's a carpenter and Ethan's an accountant. Mark's married now; it's so weird."

"They went in different directions, huh? They always seemed so similar." She sipped from her wineglass, then checked the label on the bottle. "This is good."

"Glad you like it. And yep, it's funny. They're still very close. And how about you? How about your parents?"

Hannah had only seen Angie's parents from a distance at races or in the photos Angie sent her. No matter the occasion, Angie's father always wore a suit. For her mother, it was all about dresses with matching scarfs and shawls, hair never out of place.

When Angie visited Melbourne to stay with Hannah's family all those years ago, Angie's dad sent her over and had her picked up in a separate taxi to the one he rode in. He didn't even try to meet Hannah and her folks. Viv commented on how strange she thought it was at the time; she would never let Hannah stay anywhere for so long without checking things out.

At the mention of her parents, the corners of Angie's mouth turned down. She toyed with the silver pendant on her necklace, dragging the circle back and forth. "I don't really know."

"What do you mean?"

"We're not talking. Haven't for years, actually."

"Oh, I'm sorry, that must be—"

"Yeah, rough," Angie said, reaching for her glass. "Do you mind if we talk about that another time? Kind of a long story."

The sadness in Angie's eyes was jarring, when she was always so cheerful. Whatever had happened with her parents must have really gotten to her.

"Of course. So, Neil's told me the plans for the lead-up to the Games. We'll be coming up to Brisbane in a month, right?" Hannah said.

It was the right thing to say. Angie's melancholy dropped away instantly. "That's the idea. I'm looking forward to working with you and the others on the relay strategy. I'm so excited about the team. It's going to be so good. I can't wait to see how it all comes together. It's super interesting to be on the other side of all this. I've done a little coaching over the years but nothing at this level. It's a whole different ball game. You know what I mean?"

"Can I ask you something?" Hannah's gaze followed Abdul as he deposited a bowl of fettuccine and a margherita pizza on the table between them. "Thanks, Abdul."

"You can ask me anything," Angie said, transferring noodles onto her plate. "This looks great, by the way."

"Why did you decide to join the Australian coaching team and not the American one? I mean, I'm betting you got attitude from a few of your countrymen for that decision, right?"

"Of course, I did. But I've reached the point in my life where I don't care quite so much what people think. Thankfully. People think the idea of me being a coach is a joke anyway. They assume I'm just here for decorative purposes. I'm not a *real* coach. Oh well," Angie said.

Hannah knew that feeling. There were plenty of people who thought she was trading on her name, cashing in on old glory. "That's bullshit. I bet you're a great coach. I bet you're the kind of coach who makes people feel good about the sport."

Angie smiled gently at her. "Thanks. Anyway, if you want to know the truth, I wanted to get away from the whole scene over there. I know too many people, it's all so incestuous and ugh! A lot of people were upset with me over the breakup with Trent. We knew all the same people, had a lot of the same friends. Even people who barely knew us seemed to think I was some kind of witch."

"I'm sorry to hear that," Hannah said. There was no point in pretending that she didn't know who he was. The whole world knew that Angie had married a swimmer whose fame equaled her own. "I don't understand, though, why are people upset with you? Isn't it kind of none of anyone's business?"

Angie swiped the side of her water glass with a thumb, watching the pattern she was making in the condensation. "Because we should never have gotten married in the first place. It's the biggest regret of my life."

She broke off and sipped her water, never looking at Hannah. "Well, one of them, anyway. It was foolish. But everyone loves Trent, and I'm the one who left him."

"Nobody owes anybody a relationship. If you knew you made a mistake, you had every right to leave."

While she played with her glass, she was free to observe Angie's downcast expression. It was crazy, how much she wanted to reach across the table and take her hand even though Angie had hurt her too.

There was a trail of broken hearts behind Angie, but maybe it wasn't all her fault.

"Can I take these plates for you, ladies? And would you like to see the dessert menu?" Abdul asked.

Angie's eyes lit up. "Split one?"

"Sure," Hannah said, cupping her hand around her mouth. "Don't tell anyone else on the coaching team I have no discipline."

They dipped their spoons into the layers of tiramisu, hunched close together over the bowl. Abdul had brought them share plates, which sat ignored on the table's edge.

"You know, if you factored in a race this would feel just like old times," Angie said.

"Shame you hung up your bathers. We could have swum together for old times' sake."

"That would be fun. Man, I haven't even been in a pool for so long. I miss it. Did you miss it, before?"

She decided that if Angie could open up, so could she. "I did. I missed it a lot, and I just knew I wasn't done. It was like I couldn't think about anything else. I wasn't going to be able to move ahead with my life until I gave it one more shot."

"I get that," Angie said, leaning over even further. "You know what's weird? I miss stuff I used to hate about it. I miss the smell of chlorine! Even though we used to get so upset about chlorine burns, remember that? I miss the way I'd get so hungry, it'd feel like nothing I could ever eat would be enough. Are you hungry all the time now?"

"Did you see how much pasta I just ate?" Hannah asked, patting her stomach. "You really do miss it, don't you? Why don't you swim then?"

"Well, I'd be so self-conscious, there's that. I'm way out of shape, and I'd feel like everyone was watching me."

"What about just getting in a pool for fun? You could soak yourself in that chlorine smell. It might not be the same as racing but it's something."

"I haven't done that in so long either! Maybe I'm a little scared. Who am I kidding, I'm a lot scared. If I do that, it'll all come rushing back. I was looking at the pool at my hotel this afternoon, just daydreaming about it."

Hannah wiped her mouth on her napkin and threw it onto the table. "All right, that's it. You're going to get in right now and rip off the bandage. Look at you. You're desperate to get in the water. It's right there at your hotel. Why not just get in there?"

"Right now? Isn't it a little cold for that?"

"I'm sure the pool's heated."

Angie beamed. "Do you want to come?"

"Someone has to make sure you actually do it," Hannah said, signaling Abdul for the check.

Angie's face fell. "Oh, wait. Don't get me wrong, I love this idea, but there are a couple of problems. One, I don't have my bathers, and two, look at the time. I bet the pool's closed."

"You know what that sounds like? That sounds like loser talk."

Angie threw down her napkin so that it landed next to her on the table.

"That's it. Nobody calls me chicken. Let's do this."

CHAPTER ELEVEN

Angie was staying at The Albany, one of the classic buildings on the edge of Melbourne's Central Business District. It was close enough to travel to on foot, and they walked briskly through the streets. She was humming a tune Hannah didn't recognize. They passed a church with spires reaching toward the sky. Two grizzled older men sitting on the steps paused in their conversation to wave at them.

"This is such a beautiful city," Angie said. "It's got a really nice vibe. I like it a lot."

"I know. I love it. Never thought about moving. I haven't even asked you where you're based these days when you're not coaching? I mean, when you're not here because of the Games?"

"Nowhere right now. After I retired from swimming I had this nice little Spanish bungalow in California that I lived in for a while, but I sold it because I was never there. For a few years I was picking up advertising and commentating work wherever I could get it. But now I'm footloose and fancy-free. I've got a lead on some work for when I get back to America, but I haven't nailed anything down yet."

"That's an awfully clever way of saying you're homeless."

Angie shoved Hannah hard enough to make her stumble. She cackled, righting herself.

Should she be worried about how quickly they were falling into their old dynamic? She dismissed the thought. They were old friends having a little fun. Tonight was about trying to recapture what it felt like to be teenagers, that was all. When they were younger, they'd only felt free to be silly like this with one another.

"Come upstairs? I'll get us some towels," Angie said.

"Whoa wait, who said I was getting in the pool? I meant I'd come with you and watch. I don't miss the water! I just got out of it a few hours ago. Too much water," Hannah said, shaking her head.

Angie curled her fingers around Hannah's bicep. "Are you kidding me? We're breaking into a pool, and if I get caught, I don't want it to be on my own!"

"Oh, so you want to take me down with you?"

"You bet I do. C'mon."

Soon they were at the side of the gated outdoor pool, underwater lights casting a blue glow through the water. They quietly let themselves in through the gate, Hannah pointing at the sign affixed to it, which said the pool closed at eight.

Dim lights circled the fence, and there were deck chairs along the sides. From here, they could hear sounds of horns and cars rushing by, but there wasn't a soul around.

Angie dumped the fluffy white towels onto one of the deck chairs and unfastened the strap of her shoe.

"Rookie mistake," Angie whispered, stumbling as she pulled off a heel. "I should have left these up in my room so I could run faster if anyone busts us."

Hannah sat on a deck chair to slip her shoes off, tugging her socks down and balling them together. It was only now occurring to her that she was going to be traveling home in sopping wet clothes. No taxi driver was going to let her get into their cab; she would have to climb into a tram like a drowned rat. That was the thing about being spontaneous. You had to clean up the mess afterward.

When her feet were bare and she turned back to Angie, it took a moment to register what she was seeing. Her coat and the emerald dress were pooled on the ground, kicked away along with her shoes. She looked back excitedly at Hannah and then put one hand across her lacy white bra and the other over her underwear.

"Aaaaand...I can see by your face that you did not expect me to do that. Do you want me to put it back on? I just thought that...I assumed? I wasn't about to get in the pool with that dress on. The chlorine would ruin it forever. Oh wow. I'm so embarrassed."

Hannah shook her head, smiled dumbly and looked away from Angie's thighs. Angie's hands weren't doing anything to cover her toned stomach either. With a glance, Hannah had seen the curve under her navel, the lovely slope down to her pelvis.

Abruptly, she threw off her jacket and pulled her shirt over her head. "You know what? It's not that big of a deal. It's not so different from wearing a swimsuit, right?"

"Exactly," Angie said, her gaze dipping from Hannah's face. There was no reason for Hannah to put any thought into what she wore under her clothes tonight. Thankfully she'd worn a simple black set that wouldn't be made transparent by the water.

The crisp night air prickled her skin. She carefully folded her clothes and laid them on the deck chair, pushing down self-consciousness. As she'd just said, people saw her in her bathers all the time, and this wasn't so different. A splashing sound told her that Angie was already in the pool. When she spun around, Angie was treading water and looking up at her. She was pushing wet hair back from her face, already having ducked under the water.

"Come in! It's so nice and warm in here. They must leave the heat on overnight."

Hannah made a grand entrance. She cannonballed, her heart leaping when her body smacked against the pool's surface. When she came up for air, Angie swam toward her, giggling.

"This is amazing. Thank you so much for encouraging me to do it." She pushed water back and forth, watching it sluice over her hands.

"No problem. A little light breaking and entering never hurt anyone."

"Technically we didn't have to break anything. This place was wide open."

"True."

Angie floated on her back, looking up at the sky. "Wow, those stars."

Hannah glided nearer to take in her expression. "What does it feel like, being in the water again?"

"Like I don't know how I could stand being out of it for so long? Lie down with me?"

Hannah floated next to her.

"It's so nice spending time with you again," Angie said. "You have no idea how much I've missed you."

Why did Angie say things like that? She was the one who'd ruined their relationship, and destroyed any chance of a friendship.

"Yeah. It's nice," Hannah said.

Now there was no sound but the movement of water when they kicked or changed position. She couldn't remember the last time she'd taken the time to appreciate the night sky. The stars were beautiful.

"Did you like coaching? Will you be going back to it when this is all over?"

She had put little thought into the future beyond the next six months. Everything was tied up in reviving her swimming career.

"I guess so. I couldn't ask my boss to hold my job open or anything, but I do like it. I like helping kids and getting their confidence up in the water. Sometimes I think I'd like to explore something completely different, though. I've always been good with numbers and planning, stuff like that. I've considered doing something in business, but I'm not sure. You know Marie, my friend? She works as a consultant for restaurants, and I thought something like that would be interesting. But it's hard to pick a path."

"I think you could be good at a lot of different things."

"What about you? What are your plans? Are you going to keep coaching or go back to the advertising stuff?"

"I won't be coaching forever, no. I don't know what I want to do when I grow up, like, at all. I've got ideas, but right now they seem like pipe dreams. I don't even know where I want to live."

A sideways glance revealed Angie rising out of the water, her wet white bra leaving little to the imagination.

"You'll figure it out, I'm sure," Hannah said. She rolled onto her stomach and opened her eyes, letting the chlorine sting them. It was going to be weird trying to explain this to Marie tomorrow. Maybe she'd leave out the part about being half-naked; she could almost hear Marie shrieking about it.

She stood in the water, then walked up and down the length of the pool. Up in the hotel, there were lights on in many of the rooms, making the dark ones look like missing teeth in a giant mouth. If anyone could see them down here, they weren't snitching.

"What are you thinking about?" Angie said.

She looked back over her shoulder at Angie. She was standing now, and it took all of Hannah's willpower not to stare at her chest.

"Nothing. Just wondering how the papers would report this if we got caught."

"Imagine the headlines…screw them. We can do whatever we want."

"Yeah," she said. Though she didn't believe it, it felt good to say it. "Whatever we want!"

She swam to the side, leaning back against the concrete wall behind her and spreading out her arms. From here she could see both the stars and the neon lights on city skyscrapers.

"You're not getting out, are you?"

"Nope." She kicked her legs so that they drifted in front of her.

"Good. I'm not quite ready for this to end."

Their eyes met, a wordless beat between them. Angie swam toward her, pushing hair back from her face again. She'll stop now, Hannah thought, and she said it to herself once more when Angie was only a few feet away. And then Angie was so near, moving between her legs and standing right in front of her.

Angie didn't hesitate. She spread her hands out underneath Hannah's thighs, holding her up.

"What are you doing?"

"I think you know. Do you want me to stop?" Angie asked, staying back watchfully.

When Hannah shook her head, Angie grasped her legs more firmly and leaned in, pausing with her forehead on Hannah's. Her stomach dropped. It was so different to experience this attraction as an adult, with her sexuality in full bloom.

She rested her palms on Angie's back. She glanced down between their bodies at Angie's almost bare breasts, then up again to the heat in her stare.

Angie captured her lips, mouth slick.

At first, Hannah barely kissed her back, too stunned to relax into it. But Angie's lips were so sweet as she pressed Hannah back against the pool's wall, bra-clad chest pressing into her. It made her open her mouth, kissing back hungrily.

She became untethered from any thought but that they were made to do this. They *should* do this. Angie lightly sucked on her lower lip and then slipped her tongue into Hannah's mouth.

Hannah reached down to Angie's ass, grabbing it to fit her more neatly against her. She clutched then moved forward, stepping off the wall. When she took control, Angie sighed against her, encircling her arms around Hannah's neck.

They sank into the water together, kissing with Angie's legs wrapped tightly around Hannah. Hannah's hands were on Angie's waist, thumbs stroking against soft skin. Angie's tongue was teasingly light in her mouth and on her lip.

She had always remembered Angie as being a good kisser, though there hadn't been much to compare it to back then. But this, this was devastatingly good.

Angie shifted back, tracing a finger over her jaw. She clenched it, trying for control.

"When are you going to ask me?"

"Ask you what?" Hannah pressed a light kiss to Angie's neck. Angie angled her head to expose her throat, and she kissed her there again. She flicked her tongue over the skin, tasting water. Angie sighed, tilting her body closer to Hannah.

"Hannah…Don't you want to know what happened? Why we…Why things stopped?"

Hannah stilled. "I figure you got cold feet. We were teenagers. You were experimenting, and you decided you didn't like it anymore. Am I getting warm?"

"That's what you think?" Angie said, frowning down at Hannah's chest absently.

"I don't know. I don't think anything. You didn't really give me much to go on."

The hold around Hannah's waist loosened, Angie's legs going slack.

Hannah needed this conversation to end. She was afraid of what Angie might tell her. It was so much easier not to think about it and focus on the way they were now. They were like the fuse on a stick of dynamite. What she wanted to do was go with Angie up to her room, kiss the water from Angie's body, and lie beneath her.

"Sorry, but I'm not sure why we're having this conversation now, of all times," Hannah said.

Angie drew away entirely, then ran her hands over Hannah's shoulders.

"I think I should go up to my room. You can leave the towel down here if you want."

"Angie, sorry if I…"

"No, I'm sorry. I shouldn't have done that. Any of that," Angie said, giving Hannah one last sad-eyed look before she swam away, pulling herself out of the water. "I just need to go. Goodnight. Thanks for inviting me to dinner."

Leaving wet footprints in her wake, Angie quietly opened and closed the gate. With hunched shoulders, she walked toward the hotel entrance. Hannah got out of the pool and hurriedly dried off, arranging the wet towel over the fence. When she put her clothes back on, she winced at the way it felt to have them over her damp underwear.

It wasn't as hard as she'd feared to get a cab. In the dark, the driver didn't notice her wet clothes.

At home in bed, Angie's words bounced around in her mind so that she couldn't sleep. An hour passed while she replayed the evening behind closed eyes.

Why had Angie kissed her like that? Was she even into women, or did she just enjoy how much Hannah had always wanted her? There had been no clues about Angie's intentions throughout their conversation over dinner. Angie hadn't said much about why she and Trent were divorced, or whether she'd dated men, women or both afterward.

Finally, she got up and padded out to her computer. Her still-wet hair clung to her skin as she stared at the screen, and then she began to type.

Okay, so tell me. What happened, Angie? Why did you go?

CHAPTER TWELVE

1987 - Melbourne

Hannah's knuckles were white from her grip on the phone, her palm sweating. The ringing tone was unceasing. On the other end, she pictured it screaming for attention, echoing through an empty house.

What if something terrible had happened to Angie? It was strange for her to find herself wishing that Angie was sick, that she was only spending a little time in the hospital.

Kids their age didn't die, or at least not very often. Still, it happened. There was a girl from school when Hannah was ten years old. One day their teacher stood in front of the class, stiff and stumbling over his words, to announce the girl was killed alongside her father. They lost control of their van on a highway in the Yarra Valley. Hannah had nightmares for weeks, had gone to her mother's room every night crying. What if this was something like that?

She dialed again, then once more.

"Hello?"

"Hel-hello?" Hannah said. Even with her spiraling negative thoughts, she'd somehow been sure Angie would answer eventually. It must be her mother.

"Who is this?" The voice was concerned, but normal enough. If your only child had died, maybe you wouldn't even be able to answer the phone.

"I'm sorry. This is Hannah. I'm a friend of Angie's. Is she at home?"

There was no sound, then a muffled quality as though Angie's mother was covering the receiver with her hand.

"Hello? Are you there?"

"Yes. I'm here, Hannah," she said in a clipped tone. "Listen, Angie can't talk to you. She needs to focus on her training right now."

"I know but…"

She rested a hand against the wall, putting all her weight on it.

The voice softened. "I'm going to ask you to not call here again, okay? My daughter doesn't want to speak to you. Do you understand me? Do you understand what I'm saying to you right now?"

Hannah dropped the receiver. Then she picked it up, closing the hamburger bun gently. Gazing around the room blankly, her eyes came to rest on the photos of Angie. Were those smiles in the pictures fake? Why didn't she want to talk to her?

That night Hannah stared into the dark, listening to one of Angie's mixtapes. First, there was dead air, then the Joy Division song, the backdrop of their first kiss. They each put that song at the beginning of every carefully curated playlist. After that, there were artists that she'd never much cared for until she met Angie. Angie loved The Bangles, Whitney Houston and Madonna, but they both liked Heart and Prince.

There was nobody she could talk to. She'd almost confided in Marie a thousand times, but she always pulled back at the last moment, terrified that she wouldn't understand. She rolled to the edge of the bed and grasped the shoebox from underneath her, excavating letters by upending it and tapping on the bottom.

After clicking on her lamp, she tugged paper from envelopes until she found the most recent notes. In the top left corner, Angie dated each one.

She spread the papers across her mattress, smoothing them with her palm. Angie's perky tone was a constant, promises and dreams laid out in the brightly colored ink of gel pens. Something must have happened to make it all change.

Viv must be right. Angie had met someone else and was too scared to tell her. It was probably a boy. The thought was gut-wrenching but still not as bad as the idea that she might lose her altogether. When even her closest friends didn't know that she liked girls, who else could she talk to about all that stuff?

She rushed to her desk drawer and grabbed the writing paper she reserved for Angie. The pages had a faint floral pattern along the edges, with matching envelopes.

Hey Angie,

I'm not sure what's going on with you. I don't know why you wouldn't talk to me on the phone. You've never done anything like that before, and I haven't heard from you for weeks.

I would just really appreciate it if you'd tell me what's up. If you want things to be different and just be friends, that's okay with me. I won't be mad and I'll understand. I'd still want to talk and hang out next time I see you. Our friendship is important no matter what.

Hannah

As soon as she dropped the letter in the mailbox, Hannah knew there would be no reply. If Angie were going to say anything to her, she would have done it by now. Still, wallowing was not an option. Every morning Hannah wished she could cocoon the blanket over her head and hide, but there was no stopping any of it. All the people in her life were so excited for her. There were too many of them to disappoint if she failed.

Three weeks passed, Angie's absence was final and total. Hannah had stopped asking her mother about the mail, unable to bear the way Viv looked at her when she did. Today Hannah gazed out of the car window, not saying anything beyond a mumbled greeting.

Her times were good today; she'd bounced back lately. No matter how low her mood was, it didn't impact her performance. Tim wound her up and propelled her through the water like she was a doll or a robot.

"Hannah? Did you hear me?"

"No, what?"

They were stopped at a traffic light, giving Viv time to stare at her. Two deep creases showed between her eyebrows.

"I have some news…"

She swiveled so that her seatbelt cut into her. A car horn made them jump. The light was green, and the car lurched forward.

"Well honey, we've been planning something for a while, but I didn't want to tell you until we knew for sure. We've been saving, and we got a decent tax return this year. I'm going to come to Seoul!"

"Oh my god, really? No way!" Hannah said. Not thinking it was even a remote possibility, she'd been careful not to express the wish that her mother should be there.

Viv smacked her hands against the steering wheel. "Can you imagine? I've never even been overseas before! You know, the girls at work even took up a collection to help out?"

The road in front of them grew watery. Hannah wiped her face on her sleeve. Taking one hand off the wheel, Viv reached over and ruffled her hair. "I know how homesick you get, kiddo. I'll be right there this time. I'm so proud of you, and I can't wait to watch you do your thing."

"Thanks, Viv. I'm so glad you're coming."

"Well, I know I won't get to see a lot of you, but I'll get to see you in your big races, and that's what counts. You'll know I'm there."

"Exactly. Can I sit with you on the plane?"

"You don't want to sit with your team?"

"No, I want to sit next to you."

Every time Hannah thought about the Games, a knot tied itself in her stomach. She pictured Angie freezing her out, or worse, saying why she'd stopped liking her. Though she wanted to know, she couldn't bear the idea of hearing Angie say she didn't like girls.

At least maybe the dreams would stop afterward. In a recurring nightmare Hannah dove for coins in the bottom of a murky pool, aware that Angie was there and trying to grab the same prizes. It was never-ending, silver and bronze circles reappearing when she'd cleared them all. In the morning, loss and dread clung to her.

"Hannah, can I ask you something?"

She figured out a while ago that Viv's career as a social worker taught her certain tricks, like asking for permission every time she was going to say something upsetting.

"What is it, Mom?" she asked, her happiness about Viv coming to the Games disappearing. She scowled out the window.

"Don't 'Mom' me. I just want to know…You haven't mentioned your friend in a few weeks. I've noticed you don't write to one another at all anymore. Can't remember the last time you asked me to post a letter. What's that all about? Did you girls have a fight?"

She shrugged. "Don't know."

"Well, it's a stressful time, and things can change quickly…"

"When you're my age? I know. You said all that already."

"I'm just telling you, love, I know it's upsetting when things change, but a fair-weather friend is no friend at all. You'll know a lot of people in your life, and trust me, only a handful of them will be keepers."

She hated being lectured. "Listen, not many people understand what all of this is like! Don't you get it? I love Marie and Debbie, but it's not like either of them are going to the Games."

"I know. You and Angie had a special bond, I could see that. But nobody really knows what it's like for other people, that's what empathy is for. Remember that talk we had about empathy?"

She rolled her eyes. "Yeah, I remember, you say that like we only ever had one."

"You can talk to your friends about it, and you can talk to me. We don't know what it's like, but we can still support you. Marie and Debbie are great friends. They're the type of people who'll be in your life for the long haul. They'll be like what Claire is for me."

"Oh so, when we're in our forties and fifties, we're going to hang out drinking red wine and complaining about our jobs?"

"If you're lucky, yes. So now that we're talking about it, tell me. Do you feel strange about racing this girl you were so close to?"

She bit her thumbnail. "To tell you the truth, I do feel a bit strange about it. I always beat Angie. She's a good sport about it, but I don't know. I always got the feeling that deep down it bothered her."

Viv drove on for another minute or two. She pulled abruptly off the main street, then rounded a corner. The car stopped. Undoing her seat belt, Viv twisted her body so that they were facing one another.

She looked so serious. Had she figured out the truth about Angie?

"Okay, I want you to promise me something. You're always worrying about other people, not wanting to do the wrong thing. It's okay to put yourself first for once," Viv said.

She opened and closed the buckle of her seat belt. "What do you think I'm going to do, throw the race or something? Quit worrying. It'll be fine."

She could never tell Viv how much she'd thought about it. When Angie was visiting, it was easy to clock where she was in the water and lag, just a little. She was careful not to make Angie suspicious, but she did it just enough to level the playing field. The temptation to control the outcome was greater now that Angie wasn't talking to her. If she let Angie win, would it increase the chances of Angie liking her again?

Viv frowned at her, resting her head back against the seat. "You've worked so hard for this. Just promise me you'll try to tune everything out and do your best. I'll be proud of you whether you win or not, but you're going to remember that day for the rest of your life."

When she didn't answer right away, Viv took her by the shoulders as she waited for an answer.

Hannah nodded back to her, swallowing hard. "Okay. I hear you."

CHAPTER THIRTEEN

1988 Olympic Games - Seoul

Not many sixteen year olds had traveled as much as she had, but Hannah was ignorant about the world and the places she'd been. When she was inside the walls of stadiums and sports villages, she could be anywhere.

On the way to the Olympic Village she and Viv went directly from the airport to the accommodation, only viewing the streets of Seoul from the window of a taxi. The village was a universe unto itself; everything about it impressive. The gates stood inside a large stone sculpture, spotless paved mini-streets leading away from it. Flags of every color fluttered in the wind from atop tall white poles.

She had her own room, stark white with a comfortable mattress and a bathroom she shared with Miranda Tildora. They were on the relay team together, and Hannah found the older girl intimidating. With her big brown eyes, Miranda reminded her of Whitney Houston.

When they passed in the hall, Miranda slapped her with limp high-fives. Sometimes she said, "Go Dolphins" in a tone that could be genuine or could be naked sarcasm, Hannah had no idea.

There was no competition for the first week. Though most of the athletes were gathered in Seoul, this time was carved out for them to move through the jetlag. Hannah spent her days warming up and priming herself to perform. And of course, she was preparing to see Angie.

She spent time with her mother when she could. Viv breathlessly filled her in about the sights, talking about the fantastic sliced beef and stew she'd eaten. She'd filled countless rolls of film with Buddhist temples and picturesque mountains. Hannah was already dreading the slideshows that might happen when they got home, but Viv's excitement lifted her spirits. Even if she didn't win a medal, her mom would be taking happy memories with her.

On the fourth morning at breakfast, Hannah left the counter with her tray. She stopped when someone crashed into her path. First, she saw Tony's white sneakers, then the oversize yellow basketball shorts that came down past his knees. His face and shoulders were reddened, sunburn standing out against his pale, freckled skin.

In the dining hall, Hannah always walked around with her headphones shielding her like armor. Casting her gaze downward, she pretended that if she couldn't see anyone, then they couldn't see her either.

She tried to walk around him so she could get back to hiding, but he wouldn't get out of the way. She pushed his chest, which was like trying to move a brick wall. Over the last two years, they'd developed something between friendship and rivalry. He was one of the country's top male swimmers, and she was one of the top females. They were always at the same events, but they were never going to be close.

When he still didn't budge, she yanked her headphones off. "What do you want, Tony?"

"'Ello 'ello 'ello," he said, looking pleased with his fake British accent. "What do we 'ave here?"

"Breakfast?" she replied, nodding her head toward her tray. "That's the morning meal, so I've heard."

"Right you are. You didn't sit with us on the plane. I've barely seen you since we got here. So, I've been pondering, how's your head?" he asked, tapping his temple. "Got it in the game or not?"

"Of course, I do. I always do. My mom came with me. That's why I didn't sit with you guys."

He mimed searching behind Hannah. "But your mommy's not here now, is she? You're not hiding her under your shirt? Want to sit with us now?"

"Thanks, but I just want to chill out and be by myself."

"Okay lezzo, sit by yourself then," he said, sticking out his tongue crudely before he finally shuffled past her.

"All right, dickhead," she muttered.

It wasn't the first time he'd called her that word. Had he figured out that she really was a lesbian, or was he just doing it to get under her skin? There was something oddly friendly about how he used it. It was confusing, but she never reacted or asked him about it. She was nowhere near telling anyone about how she felt, but she had made a promise to herself that she wouldn't outright deny it.

She looked around for a table where she could be alone. If she turned the music up loud enough, she might forget where she was for a while. She almost dropped her tray. Angie. She had been right behind them, and she might have heard everything he said. Angie stared at Hannah with her eyebrows knitted together, shifting from foot to foot.

Her hair was an inch longer than it had been when they'd last seen one another. It was hard to tell because of the oversize orange sweatshirt she wore, but she looked like she had lost some weight too.

Was she going to say nothing, not a word? When Hannah tipped involuntarily toward her, Angie took a small step back. It was like she thought Hannah was sick, and that she might catch it.

Hannah shook her head and dumped her tray down on the nearest table. She managed to make it back to her room before the hot angry tears fell.

* * *

During the opening ceremony for the Games, Hannah told herself how lucky she was to be part of this. Be here, she admonished herself. Really be here.

Witnessing the passing of the torch was surreal, and for a moment she was able to sink into it, a lump in her throat. She imagined her friends watching it on TV all the way back in Australia, and her mother watching her right now from up in the stands.

* * *

Three days later Hannah's eyes flew open. It was the first day of competition, and her queasiness wasn't necessarily unpleasant. It just meant that she was ready for the two-hundred-meter heat, and the races that would follow from there.

Staying in bed, she kept her legs elevated as Tim had told her to. She stared at the ceiling, marveling at how calm she felt. When she got up, she was a warrior readying for battle, stretching her arms over her head then punching the air.

Miranda emerged from the bathroom as she approached it. They nodded coolly at one another.

"Kick some ass today 'lil fish," Miranda said.

"You too."

Before she walked into the sports complex, she took a second to stare up at the majesty of the entrance and the iconic intertwining rings. Everyone knew what those rings meant. Fixing them in her mind, she thought about what Viv had said that day in the car.

I will remember this day forever.

The heat belonged to her, and she progressed to the next round. When it was time for the semifinal, she stood on the block, her focus razor sharp. She was grateful that Angie was in a different semi; it made everything simpler. In a roped-off area by the pool, Viv watched with her hands clasped under her chin. She had no intention of letting her mother down.

She dove, letting her mind empty. She shot through the pool like a cannonball. When she was out of the water, her mother hugged her so tightly Hannah could feel her chest pounding.

Viv grabbed onto her upper arms. "You made it! You made it!"

Hannah burrowed into the safety of the embrace, closing her eyes.

After lunch that afternoon, she sat with Tim for a few minutes to go over the strategy for the big race, though she knew everything by heart. How could she fail to have it by now when he'd drummed it into her so thoroughly?

"I think your biggest problem's going to be the other young girl, really," Tim said, rubbing a hand over his chin. "The American. It's always the bloody Americans!"

"Do you mean Angie Thompson?"

"Yeah, her. You've probably heard how good her qualifying times were. And she did well in the heat this morning. She's the one to beat."

"I'm not worried about her," Hannah said, chin jutting out. "I beat her at the world championships. I know I can take her."

The next morning it was easy to avoid Angie in the marshaling area, but Hannah was aware that she was only a few steps away. She rotated her arms in circles, melting off nervous energy. She knew how to do this; all she had to do was get in the pool and swim. She'd done it a thousand times, and if she didn't let it all get into her head, this didn't have to be any different.

When she looked up from staring at the ground, their eyes caught, and Hannah looked away quickly.

Angie's eyes were wide, her shoulders rounded. In another world, Hannah would be comforting her right now.

Their lanes were next to one another's. As they walked to the pool, Angie was a few short paces away. Hannah breathed deeply, trying to keep her nerves in check as they were introduced. She waved to the spectators when she heard the announcer saying her name, then sought out her mother to anchor her.

Angie and Hannah stood side-by-side as the rest of the competitors stepped up to their blocks. Once, Angie confessed to a terror about jumping the gun. It was the most awful thing Hannah could imagine. The thought drew her taut as a bow-string, and she willed her muscles to loosen.

She still didn't know what she was going to do. Despite Angie's coldness, thoughts of throwing this race had never gone away. No matter how hard she tried, she couldn't stop caring about her. Even if Angie didn't want her anymore, she still wished more than anything for Angie to be happy.

Angie cared about all this stuff so much more than she did. Plus, winning an Olympic gold medal would only draw more attention toward Hannah; the kind of attention that Angie was so much better at dealing with.

"Good luck," Angie whispered.

Hannah looked sideways at her. Was Angie speaking to her, or to the girl on Angie's other side?

Angie stared at the water, but a moment later when Hannah did the same, Angie touched her. It was so slight it could be accidental, but Hannah was sure that it wasn't. And a moment later, Angie pressed her pinkie to Hannah's.

When the first beep sounded their hands fell away from one another's, and they crouched, waiting for the next. In the seconds after she hit the water, Hannah made her decision, that is she made none. Angie might be a stranger now, but still, she knew her better than many other people did. When Angie said good luck, she'd meant it.

It was enough.

She stopped thinking and allowed her body to do what came naturally to it. She swam, knowing she would accept whatever outcome that followed.

It was only on the last lap that she realized how badly she wanted it. Though her energy was waning and the lactic acid buildup in her legs was like fire, she pushed until her fingertips met the wall.

She looked at the board in disbelief, trying not to show it. Angie had done it. She'd taken first place, and Hannah was a few tenths of a second behind her.

It wasn't supposed to happen this way. Angie was a great swimmer, but she'd always beaten her. She kept her fingers on the wall for a long time.

Angie reached across the lane divider, shaking her hand. Hannah wanted to hug her, but she turned to the next lane. Cameras were trained on them.

Next to one another on the dais, Hannah was outside of her body. She watched as a gold medal was placed around Angie's neck, the silver hanging heavily around her own.

The American anthem played, while tears streamed down Angie's face.

CHAPTER FOURTEEN

2000 - Melbourne

The night after Angie kissed her in the hotel swimming pool, Hannah waited for thirty minutes for a reply to her email. When nothing arrived, she returned to bed and passed a restless night, her pillow hard as stone with sheets tangled around her.

The next day she rose for her morning training session, sluggish from the wine and heavy food of the evening before. Her body wasn't as forgiving as it had been when she was an adolescent. In those days, she'd been able to eat whatever she wanted and still perform.

Though her body was slow, her thoughts rushed again. What did Angie mean by that kiss? Was it driven by nostalgia or genuine attraction? Hannah had already waited for so long to find out why Angie had dumped her, so this small piece of extra time should mean nothing. But Angie had dangled an explanation in front of her last night, and now Hannah was desperate to hear it.

On the way home from training, she picked up the mail from her post office box. She prepared a protein shake, then sorted through postcards and letters from strangers. Cute notes from kids were arranged into a pile for replies. She swept the hardwood floors and rearranged cushions on the sofa. Finally, she made a cup of black coffee and sat at the computer.

She leaned in close to the screen to peer at her email.

Hey. Sorry about last night. I know I acted kind of like a crazy person. I really did appreciate you inviting me out to dinner, and I'm sorry for the way I behaved. I woke up this morning feeling more embarrassed than I've ever been in my life.

I should have just come out with it, I guess. The reason why things went bad before Seoul. I still can't seem to and I don't know why. I guess because we didn't talk for so long, that now I don't know how to talk to you anymore, but I really want to.

This is a conversation I'd like to have in person. Would you mind if I came around, if you have time to spare? I promise not to jump you or anything again! I just want to talk. I'm about to head out and do some looking around and sightseeing, mainly because I need the distraction, but I'll find an Internet café in a couple of hours.

I know you're busy and I don't want you to feel pressured, but I'd love to clear the air. - A.

Hannah checked the clock in the corner of the screen. If she replied now, she might catch Angie at the Internet café.

It's okay, and yes if you could come around, that would be great. I need to be back to train in a couple of hours, but I have some time before then, and I'd really like to talk.

She added her address to the bottom of the email, then held her breath and refreshed the page until a reply loaded. Angie confirmed that she was hailing a cab right away.

Hannah paced from the entry of her apartment to the sliding door at the back, looking blankly out at the patio. The plants needed watering, and she could call Marie or Viv, but Angie wasn't far away and she didn't want to get stuck on the phone. Hannah tented her fingers behind her head as she walked the length of the apartment again.

When she heard a car pulling into her driveway, she stared at her front door. She smoothed a hand over her stomach before opening it.

Angie was reaching over to pay the driver, and Hannah watched, leaning against the doorframe. When Angie got out, Hannah looked down at her yoga pants and tank top, questioning why she hadn't thought to change her clothes while she was waiting.

Angie's white dress stopped above the knee, the loose hair flowing over her shoulders adding to her ethereal look. She pushed the taxi door behind her, not breaking eye contact.

"Hey. Thanks for letting me come over," Angie said.

"Of course. Come on in," Hannah replied, staring around to make sure none of her neighbors were in the drive.

When they were inside, Angie swept a shaky hand through her hair. "This is a nice place."

"Come on, it's okay," Hannah said, grabbing Angie lightly by the wrist and tugging her toward the sofa. It helped her to comfort Angie, distracting her from her own thumping heart.

"This is really lovely. You own this place?" Angie asked. When Hannah nodded, she rose and walked toward the sliding door. "It looks like you've got a nice garden out there. Is that an herb garden in the corner?"

"It is. I've put a bit of work into it. I like how private it is. I think I got the best house on the block. Angie, sorry, but can we get to it?"

Angie sat next to Hannah on the sofa. "I'm really sorry about last night."

"I know you are. It's okay. Let's just talk. Tell me what you wanted to tell me last night."

"Okay," Angie said. She fiddled with a coaster on the coffee table, moving it toward the edge and then back in place again. "It was my folks. They were the reason I had to stop talking to you."

"Your folks? What do you mean?"

"They found all our letters. I kept them in my room, and I thought I'd hidden them well, but Mom went digging when I was at training. I came home to find them all on the table, just spread out like…like she was investigating a crime or something. That's how they treated me. Like I'd done something unforgivable."

"Oh no," she said. The danger of the scene was laid out in her mind's eye, Angie so young and vulnerable.

"For a while, I thought they were going to send me away to one of those conversion therapy camps! Like in that movie, *But I'm A Cheerleader* or something. But of course, they could never do that when they wanted me to keep swimming. I was their cash cow. It could ruin that. They told me I was putting everything at risk, that nobody would want me for endorsements or anything if they ever found out what we were doing. When you called, they wouldn't let me speak to you. I was standing right there that day, I remember that. It was all so horrible."

Of all the scenarios Hannah had considered, this one hadn't occurred to her. Now it seemed obvious; a missing puzzle piece that she shouldn't have needed to see the whole. Angie didn't speak about her parents much, but when she did, it was clear how much they controlled her life. The idea was so foreign. Her own parents would never go through her things. They would never tell her whom she should have in her life, and they'd always given her the gift of letting her make her own mistakes.

"I'm really sorry. It was so hard not to talk to you," Angie said. "I thought about calling or writing, but they controlled everything, checked the phone bills and stuff."

Hannah was frozen, her forehead crinkling. Now there was someone to blame and rage against, someone other than Angie, but how much could it help when it was ten years later? They'd been young, but nobody stayed that way forever. Angie had access to Hannah's email address for weeks now, and a few simple sentences could have shone a light into all those dark spaces.

"You didn't try to talk to me, though? Not even when I saw you in Seoul. When we were at the village, there would have been a million ways you could have got that message through to me. You just stared at me the day that I saw you there in the cafeteria. Do you remember that?"

Angie covered her face. "Of course, I do. Like it was yesterday. You see, it wasn't so hard for them to control me from afar. And once they'd planted that shame in me, worked me over like they did…"

"It's been years, though. You couldn't have written me a letter later on? I mean, I don't want to sound like I don't care about what happened to you, it's awful. But we've been grownups for a long time now."

Angie looked Hannah in the eye. "I know I should have. I wanted to, a million times. I had a tough few years there, coming to terms with who I was. I had to deal with the fact I had a husband I never should have married. Getting divorced and coming out in my twenties was hard. I know things were hard for you too."

"They were."

"I don't know what to say. I have no excuse other than I moved on, and I told myself that you had too, and it wouldn't be fair to dredge up the past like that. I never stopped thinking about it, though. I never stopped feeling bad about it."

Hannah stood and approached the sliding door. She put a palm on the glass, seeing past her reflection to the herb garden and her back fence, strung with broken fairy lights.

When she was younger, she'd been ashamed of being gay. It took a long time for her to work her way through it, even with how supportive her parents were when she came out to them. Things had changed so much in ten years and were changing all the time. But it still wasn't easy. Her sexuality was an open secret in the swimming world, but she understood that she had to keep it relatively quiet. She spun back around to Angie.

"Okay. Thanks for telling me."

Angie wiped her cheek where a tear had fallen. "Sorry it took me so long."

"It's all right," Hannah said. "I meant what I said when we met again. We were so young. *So* young. I held on to a few things over the years, but I really do get it. Some of it anyway. It must have been tough for you, wasn't it? You didn't have what I have with my family."

"We're not really supposed to be worrying about me right now."

"Why not? Tell me about it; I want to know."

She sat down next to Angie, resting against the sofa. Keeping her distance, when she wanted to fold Angie into her arms.

"Sure, it was hard. I imagine it's hard for all teenagers, figuring this stuff out, but it was so much worse with the spotlight on me like it was. I was so paranoid! Thinking that people would be able to figure it out just by looking at me."

Hannah reached forward, wiping Angie's face. Angie caught her hand, and only let go reluctantly.

"And now? Are you okay? I mean, you said you didn't speak to your folks. Is this the reason why? Do they still not accept you?"

Angie looked toward the ceiling. "That's the tip of the iceberg with them. I don't know where to start. They controlled everything in my life until I got married, which is why I got married so young, and that was a big mistake, let me tell you. Then I found out they'd spent a large chunk of my earnings."

"Whoa. That's horrible. Why would they do that? I thought your parents were loaded?" Hannah caught herself. "Sorry."

Angie laughed. "They're the kind of people who like to look like they are, but they have no money in the bank. Not a red cent. That's why they always rode me so hard. So, I made a choice a few years ago that it would be better for me to protect myself and have some distance. I send them cards at the holidays, but that's about it."

"I'm sorry," she said again. She had always taken her close-knit family for granted. How lucky she was!

She pulled Angie into her arms, resting her chin on top of Angie's head while Angie nuzzled into her. They stayed that way for precious minutes, Hannah patting Angie's back and rubbing her smooth upper arms.

When they finally separated, Hannah grabbed a box of tissues from the coffee table. She passed them to Angie, looking away while she dabbed under her eyes.

"There's something else I thought we should talk about," Angie said.

"What? Oh! Last night."

It was a relief to see Angie laughing again. "Yeah, um..." Angie said, until Hannah jumped in.

"I'm guessing we're not really supposed to be doing that, with you being the coach and all."

"Well, no. I mean, I wanted to, obviously, but I got kind of carried away. I also don't want to do anything to distract you from the Games. I remember how intense it was, this part of the training. I'm sorry."

"It's okay," Hannah said softly. "You can stop apologizing. So, what are we going to do?"

"I don't know. What do you want to do?"

"Can I tell you something? I'm finding this all very confusing. It's so strange. Sometimes it feels like no time has passed at all since I've seen you, then other times it feels like we're totally different people. Do you know what I mean?"

"I know exactly what you mean. Right? It's weird! We never spent more than two weeks together, but I feel like I really know you? What is that about?"

"Do you think it feels weird because we got interrupted back then? Things might have naturally run their course?"

"But we never got the chance to find out? Yes. I think you might be right. God, it's such a relief to be able to talk about this," Angie said.

"It is, isn't it?"

"Really is. I mean, I never behave the way I did last night," Angie said with her hand on her chest. "I was all over you!"

"Don't you dare say you're sorry again. It takes two. Enough."

"All right, I'll try to stop. So, again, what do we do?"

"I said a while ago I thought it would be cool to get to know one another again as adults. I still think that, but now I feel like we can be a bit more honest about it. So, what do you think? Do you want to be friends for real?"

"More than anything. Can I please see you again before I go? I know you're busy, but I'd love to talk more. Can I cook you lunch tomorrow? Or dinner?"

"I'd love that. I really would."

CHAPTER FIFTEEN

Hannah ran on the treadmill, staring up at the television suspended over the machines. The talking head on the screen, a blond woman with a square jaw, had interviewed her a few times. Reporters always looked so different when you saw them in person.

Over the silent movement of the reporter's mouth, an Elvis Costello song played through her headphones. While she watched, she mused over the fact that Angie would be at her house again in an hour.

The anger and bewilderment that had lived in Hannah for so long didn't have a home anymore. All she felt was excitement at the thought of spending time with Angie again.

At her apartment, Hannah rinsed off sweat and chlorine. It was almost time for Angie to arrive and she still had to do something about her hair. It hung around her face, stringy and damp. She couldn't remember the last time she'd blow-dried it.

She rummaged around in the cupboard under the sink, cocking her head. The bathroom was on the second level, and she thought she'd heard a knocking on the front door at the bottom of the stairs. A moment later there was a gentle tapping.

"Shit!" she said, reaching for the robe on the back of her bathroom door. It had an ugly paisley pattern on it, but it had been a gift from Viv, and she liked the soft fabric. She glanced at herself in the mirror and decided that she looked so bad she could only laugh about it.

As she opened the door, she pulled the belt tighter around her waist. Angie was bright and summery, standing on her small porch in her brown leather sandals and a sky-blue sundress.

"Hey."

Angie paused, a grocery bag clutched in each hand. Her gaze dragged up and down Hannah's body, her eyes wide. "Sorry. Did I get the time wrong?"

"No! My bad, time got away from me. Come on in. Here, let me take one of those."

Their fingers brushed when Hannah took a bag and Angie followed. Hannah set the bag down on the white marble kitchen island.

"Do you mind if I…" Hannah said, gesturing upstairs.

"Of course! Can I get started on dinner? I'm going to make us tofu and sweet potato curry. Does that sound okay?"

"That's perfect. Help yourself to anything you need. I won't be long."

There wasn't time to do anything about her hair, but she put on some mascara and lip gloss, then dressed in a loose button-up white shirt. She wasn't used to the noises of someone puttering about in the kitchen, pans rattling and the fan over the hotplate whirring.

"Can you find everything okay down there?" she called.

"I've got this, don't worry!"

She zipped up her jeans. On the steps, she lingered to observe Angie moving around her kitchen, her feet bare. At the island where Angie had laid the chopping board, she sliced onion in smooth strokes.

"Can I help with anything?" Hannah asked, finally descending the last few steps.

"Thanks, but I'm good. Why don't you take a load off? You must be tired from training all day," she said, pointing with the knife toward the stool at the island.

Angie pushed a glass of ice water toward her, which included a wedge of lemon. "Here. Hydrate."

"Jeez, I could get used to this."

"I'm here one more day, so I could come over and cook dinner for you tomorrow night too if that's not too much? It's nice to have the company when you travel as much as I've been doing."

"You're very welcome if you don't mind waiting on me. So, how do you like hanging out in Melbourne? What did you do today?"

"I went to the art gallery. There are some great permanent collections there. Saw the aquarium, too, and then I just sat around having coffee and people watching. It's fun being a tourist. I almost don't want to go back to Brisbane, but we've got lots of strategy sessions coming up." She went to the stovetop, carefully setting out everything she'd need.

"You like cooking, don't you?"

Angie took a band from around her wrist and tied back her hair, uncovering the long column of her neck. "I do. I find it super meditative. Know what I mean? It really takes my mind off anything I'm worried about. I love finding new recipes and making my own adjustments and everything. Plus you get to eat something delicious at the end. Well, hopefully. I like cooking vegetarian dishes too. It makes me a bit more creative."

"I'm sure this will be delicious. It already smells so good."

The scents of frying onion, garlic, and spices filled the room. Angie glanced back over her shoulder while she stirred. When their eyes locked, Hannah looked away, picking up her water glass.

They sat down to eat at Hannah's small round table. She'd always loved this table, a walnut top with white legs. When she was upstairs, Angie had set it with cloth napkins and a jug of water.

Hannah unfolded her napkin, admiring the embroidered pattern around the edges. "Where did you get these? Did you bring them over?"

"They're yours but you don't know what you have in your kitchen, do you?"

"You have me there. I eat a lot of eggs, make a lot of protein shakes and stuff. But I don't entertain very much. They've probably been wherever you found them for years. My ex might have bought them. She was into entertaining."

Angie's hands slowed in their work. "Oh, right."

"You're a good cook, Angie," Hannah said after another bite. "You can for sure come over to make me dinner again!"

"Glad you like it. I've been toying with the idea of getting into something food related for a while. Like starting or joining a catering company, training as a chef or something like that. I don't know exactly what yet. I just can't see myself being involved with the swimming world for the rest of my life, you know?"

"You should do it!"

"Maybe one day. So…Are you with someone now?"

Hannah coughed, a chunk of sweet potato almost caught in her throat. Did Angie really think they'd have kissed if she was already in a relationship? Of course, some people did things like that, but she'd always been strictly monogamous.

"Excuse me. No, I'm single. Haven't met anyone I've liked for a while now. Doesn't help that I've got photographers following me around, and I don't want the press to know too much about my personal life. My love life is a bit of a mess, I guess."

"And your ex, the one who bought the napkins. Did she live here?"

"No, she didn't live here. I mean, it was serious. We were together for a couple of years, but I've never lived with anyone. Is that weird?" Hannah asked, screwing up her nose. According to Marie, she was a commitment-phobe. According to herself, she just liked her own space and company.

Angie smirked. "You're weird, sure, but not for that reason."

She laughed. "How am I weird?"

"I don't know, you were just always a little different. You march to the beat of your own drum. It's what I always liked about you."

"Now, your turn," she said, flushing at the compliment.

"Oh shit, what?"

"What's the story. What was it like with Trent?"

When Angie grimaced, Hannah scrambled to cover. "Sorry, I know you're divorced. I guess it's not the nicest topic for you."

"No, it's okay," Angie said, touching Hannah's hand. "I honestly don't know what I was thinking. I was just trying to do all the right things like my parents wanted. The husband, the house. I'm so thankful we didn't get as far as having kids! When I look back, I can see I always had one foot out the door. It would have been a disaster if we'd stayed together. At least we made a clean break. Or, as clean as it gets when your ex hates you, anyway."

"Don't worry, I'm pretty sure some of my exes hate me as well."

"You hated me too, didn't you?" Angie said, gamely meeting her eye. "Before I told you what happened?"

"Don't be silly, I didn't hate you. I mean, it hurt, but like I keep saying, we were just kids. It's crazy that we're even still talking about it. How long were we together, like a month or something? And we didn't even spend a lot of time in the same place!"

"We were together for three months, but it felt like longer to me," Angie said, not smiling. "I think we would have been together for a long time if my parents hadn't involved themselves."

Hannah sobered. "I always thought that too. Even though we lived in different countries. So what about long-term stuff for you, anyway? Have you been with anyone since Trent?"

"Sure, I had a girlfriend for a while. I met her in California, she's a nurse. It was hard with me moving a lot after I retired. I don't think she really got it. I think the two of us being swimmers had a lot to do with us being so tight. Don't you think?"

"Yep. Maybe your parents figured out how close we were from our letters, and that's why they freaked out so much?"

"Probably, sure. But I wouldn't know, because those jerks threw out all your letters."

"Oh no, not my masterpieces!"

"You can joke, but I was really upset! I still got to keep that watch, though. I never told them you gave it to me."

"The mermaid watch?"

"That's right, I still have it in fact."

"Holy shit. Were you wearing it the first day you came and saw me in Bondi? I thought I saw something."

"I was. Do you think that's strange?" Angie said, searching her face.

"Not at all. I've still got all your letters." Hannah pointed above her head. "They're in a shoebox up there."

"Oh wow, can I see them? I have to see them," Angie said, fists clenched in front of her mouth. "I'm terrified. Do you think you could get them, please?"

Hannah scooped up the last mouthful of curry, then scraped back her chair. She ran up the stairs, grabbing the box from a shelf in the built-in wardrobe in her spare room. As she was moving a box out of the way, she heard water running downstairs.

"Don't you do the dishes! You cooked, I'll do them later," she said, working the shoebox out from under a pile of bags. It was the same box she'd always stored her letters in, covered with faded pictures of celebrities she'd cut out of magazines and pasted to the sides.

"I haven't opened this box for years. Not since before Seoul," she said, breathless from running down the stairs so fast. She handed it to Angie, who carried it toward the living room like it was a precious artifact.

"I had a special box too, you know. It was this carved wooden thing I'd bought at an antique store. I got so mad at my parents I broke it! Smashed it into pieces. What a drama queen."

Hannah sat beside her on the sofa as Angie set the box on the coffee table and removed the lid. She selected a random envelope and took out the folded piece of paper, leaning back against the sofa. Hannah watched her eyes move back and forth across the page.

"'I think about you all day every day and everything I do it just feels like I'm waiting to see you again.' Wow, we were pretty intense, huh? Or at least, I was."

"Oh, I was right there with you. You might not have the letters, but I remember that."

Angie dropped the letter onto the coffee table, red-cheeked and scowling.

"Maybe this wasn't such a good idea. If I'd known it was going to upset you, I wouldn't have gotten them out."

Hesitantly, she rested a palm on Angie's knee. Angie put her hand on top of Hannah's. "I'm not upset. I'm angry. My parents stole so much from me. My money, you…I thought I'd come to terms with a lot of it, but I'm still so mad at them."

"And why shouldn't you be? It's normal that you're angry. Rage away. But it didn't last forever. You're sitting here with me, right now."

A smile lightened Angie's face. "That's right. I'm not a teenager anymore. I can do whatever I want. I'm free from them. They can't control me anymore."

"That's right. Screw them!"

"Yeah! Fuck you, Mom, fuck you, Dad!"

They were both giggling now, and Angie yelled, beating her chest. "That feels so good to say. It feels good to let it out."

Hannah grabbed her in a hug.

They sat holding one another, hearts beating as one.

CHAPTER SIXTEEN

The next day, Hannah set aside extra time to make herself presentable, going home early to prepare for dinner with Angie. It meant skipping the massage she had booked, but she didn't mind.

In the shower, she sang "Love Will Tear Us Apart." It was her favorite song once, but she hadn't listened to it for years. All day she had looked forward to tonight—a tasty dinner and good conversation with Angie.

Somehow caught again, she heard the door opening while she was pulling a form-fitting black shirt over her head. At least she'd already found time to dry her hair.

In her rush to get up here, she must have forgotten to lock the door. It was strange that Angie would just let herself in like that, but maybe she'd been knocking for a while, and Hannah hadn't heard. She jogged toward the top of the stairs.

"Hey!" she said, halting when she saw the top of a head with black curly hair. "Oh, hey. Marie."

"Hey, hey! I knocked off work early so I thought I'd drop by and…Where are you going?"

"Nowhere," she said, checking her watch. She walked down the stairs, knowing that she had precisely fifteen minutes to get Marie out of here. "Just took a shower after getting back from training, that's all."

"You look good. Are you sure?" Marie said, one eyebrow arched.

"Yeah…listen, I'm expecting company."

At that, Marie walked further into the apartment, dropping her red handbag on the entry table. She sat down at the dining table and tented her fingers. "Lady company. I can tell. All right, spill. I'll leave as soon as you tell me who's coming over."

She sighed, settling onto a chair across from her. "It's Angie. It's no biggie. She's just coming around to hang out and cook some dinner."

Marie slapped her palms onto the table, her fingers splayed as she leaned as close to Hannah as possible. "After you just went out for dinner together the other night? You never called to fill me in like you were supposed to, which now strikes me as suspicious. You're seeing her a lot. Tell me what's going on?"

She rechecked her watch. "We can talk, but I really need you to head off in fifteen minutes. Ten to be safe."

"You can say a lot in ten minutes. Go."

"Well, when we went out for dinner, I found out that she was staying through the weekend and had nothing to do. So, I invited her over. She ended up finally telling me the reason she stopped writing to me and cut off contact and all that. It was because of her parents. They made her do it."

"Hmmm," Marie said, sitting back with her arms crossed.

"Hmm, what?"

"Nothing. Ugh, look, I guess I just think that's a bit lame. Don't you think Angie could have found a way to tell you that? It's been, what, ten years? And she only tells you this now? I don't like it. No. I don't like it at all."

"What do you mean you don't like it? Don't you see that I've been waiting for all this time to find out what actually happened and now I know?"

"Right, I'm sorry, girl. But what am I supposed to say?"

"I don't know," Hannah said, sinking down in her chair. "Some support would be nice."

Marie grabbed her hand. "Babe. You lost a gold medal because of her. This is the worst possible timing for you to get interested in her again. Do you really want to blow your big comeback on your high school girlfriend?"

"I didn't lose because of her. I know I threw everything I could at that race. She was faster than me that day. Sometimes, you just don't make it. I can't hold her responsible for that."

"With respect, that's bullshit. Maybe you didn't consciously let her win, but it affected you. I saw how sad you were back then even if I was in the dark about a lot of stuff. I knew she'd ditched you, but I had no idea you were in love with her. God, I still remember when you told me. I wanted to fly over there and punch her in her face."

"Aw, you're such a good friend, threatening violence like that. I know, I was super sad. But I was a teenager, dramatic like only kids can be. I'm okay now, and I'm okay with her."

"Don't you think it's a bit weak, though?"

She used her hands to cradle one of Marie's. "I thought so at first, but then I remembered a few things about my own stuff. You've always been so supportive of me, so I don't want you to take this the wrong way. But you don't know what it's like to be that young and to know that you like girls."

"So?"

"So, her parents did a number on her. They would have planted the seed that she was sick and wrong, and all the other things people say. I think they started the job, but she finished it herself. She was ashamed. And that's not her fault. I can't stop thinking about the fact that she ended up in a marriage with a man, when she didn't want it. That's like a prison."

Marie withdrew her hand, patting Hannah's. "All right. I'll get out of your hair. You make a decent case. But if she does anything to hurt you, I really will punch her this time. Right in the boobs."

"Thanks. I love you. Now get out," Hannah said, waving toward the door.

She walked Marie to her car, giving her a quick hug before playfully pushing her into it. As soon as Marie's hatchback pulled out of the driveway, a silver top taxi pulled into it. Hannah bounced on the balls of her bare feet while Angie paid the driver.

"Did you just have a guest? I hope they didn't leave on my account!" Angie said, slamming the taxi door shut behind her. She walked up, and they stood, open smiles reflecting one another's.

"It was Marie, she just dropped by. Come on inside."

"Have I said how much I love your house? It's so light and lovely. You've decorated it so beautifully too. It must be great to come home to this every day."

She looked around, trying to see the apartment through Angie's eyes. The newest item she'd bought was a blue and red striped rug laid over the polished wooden floorboards, and it gave the room just the right amount of color.

"I am happy here. It's nice to be reminded to appreciate it. So, what delightful dish will I be served tonight?" she asked, draping herself over the island counter.

Angie put her elbows on the counter. "Tonight, I'll be cooking black bean and squash enchiladas. I hope you like Mexican food?"

"Are you kidding, I love it. But let me help you this time."

"All right. You can be my sous chef. You start by cutting up the squash, that's my least favorite part."

"Sure. I can do your dirty work."

"Thanks," Angie said, unloading vegetables and tins from a bag.

Hannah wrestled with peeling the skin from the squash, gripping the handle of the knife and pushing it down as hard as she could. "Jesus, I see why you hate this."

"Well, thanks for doing it. Should we listen to some music, do you think?"

"Sorry, I don't have any Debbie Gibson."

"I have *never* liked Debbie Gibson."

Hannah smirked. "Whatever you say."

Once upon a time, she'd been partial to the cheesy eighties' pop star, but she'd never tell Angie that. She pointed toward the CD player and disc collection with the tip of her knife. "Help yourself."

Angie crouched, rifling through the plastic cases. While her back was turned, Hannah admired the way her muscles stood out on her calves, her skirt revealing the lovely shape of her thigh.

Eventually, she settled on a blues collection Hannah had found years ago in a dollar bin at a chain store. She couldn't remember if she'd ever listened to it, but when the opening notes of a Motown song played, she bopped her head to the beat.

"Good choice," Hannah said. "I like the old stuff."

"See, I can have good taste, Miss Cool. I bet you were one of those people who liked Nirvana before anyone knew who they were. Weren't you?"

When she was in her late teens, Hannah introduced her little brothers to grunge music, and they'd all flipped over it. "There might have been a few flannel shirts in my closet. Hey, I'm done with this. What's my next task, boss?"

"Can you please fry up this onion and garlic? Then I'll pass you stuff. We're making the sauce."

She took the box she kept by the oven and struck a match to light the gas hotplate, then shook some oil into a pan. She waited for it to heat up, periodically putting her palm over the top to check. She couldn't remember the last time she'd cooked with someone like this. Angie passed her a bowl of chopped onion, then bustled around behind her.

Angie put a hand on her arm, leaning to peer over her shoulder. "I think that's soft enough. Garlic time, here."

Hannah stirred it into the pan, leaning over and inhaling deeply. "I love the smell of garlic. So, when do you head back to Brisbane exactly? I can't remember if you said tomorrow or the next day?"

It was so quiet that Hannah repeated the question, glancing back to see Angie near her again. She passed her a small bowl of ground spices, gesturing that Hannah should tip it into the pan.

"I fly out in the morning."

"Oh. But who's going to cook my dinner?" Hannah cracked.

Angie didn't reply. A moment later she was next to Hannah, a hand on her as she reached around to pass her a can of pureed tomato. "Are you supposed to be a comedienne or a sous chef? I can't tell."

The voice close to her ear, low and soft, made Hannah shiver. She poured the tomato into the pan, then worked it around, Angie's hand lingering at her hip for a moment longer.

"I'd like to think that I can be both," she said, fighting the urge to turn in Angie's arms. She forced her attention back to the pan.

When they were ready to eat, Angie placed small bowls of cilantro and toasted pepitas on the table. She added a bottle of hot sauce and salsa and then fussed with the placement of everything before she sat down.

"We made a good team, sous chef," Angie said.

"We did," Hannah agreed. Under the table, she pulled her foot back from where it brushed against Angie's.

After dinner, Hannah washed the dishes and Angie insisted on drying them.

"So, do you remember a guy called Tony from my team?" Hannah asked, plunging a plate into the water.

"I think so? The red-haired guy, right? Why do you ask?"

"He's huge here now. He hosts this cheesy gameshow called *Not That Door*, and he has this advice talk show thing too."

"That's so funny. If only we'd managed to parlay our swimming careers into B-grade celebrity shows, right?"

Angie hung her red dishtowel on the bar over the stove, glancing around the kitchen to check that there was nothing else to do.

"I feel bad about all the stuff you bought. You can't exactly take the condiments with you on the plane."

"No problem, I wanted to do it. You can have it with the leftovers."

"I'll ration out those leftovers like nobody's business. Those and the curry from the other night will keep me going for days."

"Good. So, I guess I'll see you in Brisbane?" Angie asked brightly, but her smile didn't reach her eyes.

"If you're not too tired, I can make us some herbal tea? I'm still feeling pretty wired."

"Sure!"

They sat on opposite ends of the sofa facing one another, holding mugs of tea with their legs bent, feet almost touching.

"So. I've told you a thing or two about me, and my ex-husband and parents and all. Now it's your turn to spill the beans," Angie said, blowing on the top of her tea.

"An interrogation wasn't what I had in mind when I suggested tea!"

Angie extended her leg, her foot bumping Hannah's shin. "Nothing to be scared about. I just want to know more about what it was like after we…after I stopped talking to you. You were still swimming for a while after that, but then your retirement seemed kind of abrupt. So, there's a lot I don't know about what was happening with you. From the outside it seemed like you were at the top of your game."

"It might have looked like that from the outside, sure."

"I thought I was going to see you at Barcelona. I was so upset when I found out you'd retired."

"I was planning on going. I quit during training."

Angie hadn't moved her foot. She pressed it more firmly against Hannah's jeans, their eyes locking. "Tell me?"

CHAPTER SEVENTEEN

1991 - Melbourne

Training for Barcelona was all-consuming, giving shape to the aimlessness of her life since she'd graduated high school.

As much as she wanted to support her friends, most of whom had gone on to university, she was stuck with this feeling. Left behind. The transition out of high school was confusing; she hadn't known how much she would miss it. Nothing replaced school when she graduated except for the mounting swimming commitments. Now it felt like the sport was all that she was.

She went through the preparation just as she had for every other significant event. Tim tailored their sessions toward competition, becoming more rigid and short-tempered by the day.

She trained at the same aquatic center as Tony, and they often met for breakfast after their morning laps. He could be obnoxious sometimes, but it helped to hang out with someone who was a similar age. It gave her something to do while the rest of her friends went to class, partied and slept late.

This morning they dined in a café across the street from the pool; sparsely decorated, with a Russian waiter who was always smiling. He loved talking to them about swimming.

Hannah attacked her three-egg omelet with salmon on the side. She sipped black coffee, savoring the bitterness.

"I don't know how you can drink that shit," Tony said, shoveling buttered toast into his mouth. He could consume a slice in a couple of bites.

"Lucky it's mine and not yours then."

"Very lucky. So. My times were excellent this morning. I can't wait for Barcelona. I look forward to adding new medals to my trophy case."

"You're such a wanker. Is that how you get girls to have sex with you? You show them your trophy case?"

He slanted his eyes. "Woman, look me in the eye and tell me that you're doing this for the love of it and no other reason. Tell me you don't care about medals. Tell me you don't want to scoop up a gold."

She held up her forefinger and thumb. "All right, maybe just a bit."

"Hey. Can I ask you something?"

"You can try. I can't guarantee I'll answer," she said. It wasn't like him to ask for permission for anything. If it was about her love life, she might throw her fork at him.

"Do you ever get sick of the way Tim talks to you? He can be pretty harsh."

This morning Tim had lectured her poolside about her performance. What bothered her about it the most was that her times were just as good as they'd ever been. Better. But it was never good enough. Nothing would stop him from pushing her to be faster and more efficient. Over the years she'd grasped the core of his coaching technique. He withheld his approval until he was sure that he'd squeezed every drop from her.

In recent months, especially since she was swimming full-time, they'd butted heads more often. She was no longer the passive twelve year old she'd been when they met.

Somewhere along the line, she came to understand that
he got his kicks out of chastising her because his days as a
competitor were long behind him. And somewhere along the
road, his drill sergeant manner grated on her so much that she
was always just a little bit angry.

She took a gulp of coffee, burning her tongue. Many coaches
could be hard on their charges, but if Tony was commenting on
it, Tim was particularly severe. Did putting up with it make her
look weak? She made a snap decision to trust Tony.

"Of course. I feel like Tim's getting worse. Have you
noticed?"

"Yep. That's why I thought I should say something. You
know, you shouldn't have to deal with his shit. He's taken you
this far, but at the end of the day, this is your career. He needs
you more than you need him."

"I never thought of it like that. What do you think I should
do? I've tried talking to him about it a million times, but he
never changes. Sometimes lately we'll have a big fight, and
he'll soften up for a day or two, then he'll be even more of an
asshole after that. Like he's taking it out on me for standing up
for myself. I try to just get on with it, but he's kind of ruining
this for me."

"Fire his ass! So many coaches would want to take you on."

"Wow. You're so nice, Tony! I didn't know you had it in
you."

He pointed a warning at her. "Don't tell anyone. And I really
think you should. Honestly, he deserves it. I've thought that for
months. You don't know how many times I've felt like stepping
in. He's a bully."

He was right. She'd allowed herself to be bullied, but the
important thing was that she could do something about it now
if she wanted to.

She promised herself that she'd talk to her folks about Tim
tonight.

"Thanks, Tony. I need to give it some thought."

That afternoon when Hannah returned to the aquatic center, the conversation with Tony was fresh in her mind. When she left the changing room, Tim was standing by the pool with a hand on his waist, the other fiddling with his beard.

"You're here! Sorry if I'm keeping you from something more important."

She checked the clock on the wall behind him. Five minutes late. She passed him and stood in position. Tony was looking at her from a couple lanes away.

"All right, let's see if you can do better than this morning," Tim said, weighted vest hanging from the hook of his index finger. "Give me twenty laps in this, and I'm going to clock each one. I want to see even pacing if you can manage it."

Wordlessly she threaded her arms through the sleeves then snapped the belt shut around her waist. She scanned for the nod to signal it was time to go, Tim's finger poised on the button of his stopwatch. The corners of his mouth twisted downward like he'd tasted something sour. He was already disappointed in her.

With each lap, her resentment grew. Why didn't he want to inspire her? Why couldn't they work together and act as a team?

After she'd counted to twenty, she paused breathlessly at the end of the lane. She could barely look at Tim, knowing that he was about to rake her over the coals.

"Get out," he said, eyes on the clock in his hand. Reaching down to the gym bag by his feet, he unzipped it and pulled out a pair of brand-new white sneakers. "Pretty sure these are your size."

"What are they for?"

"What are they for?" he mocked. "What do you think? Put them on and keep the vest on too. I want another twenty, and I'd like to see you maintain the same time you just did per lap."

She stared at the shoes. "Okay. What was my time per lap?"

"You should have a sense by now of what your times are like. What did it feel like?"

"What did it feel like? I don't…"

The shoes landed with a thud. He marched forward to get in her face, but his voice was so quiet that nobody would hear it. "You're bloody useless today. Just pick those up, put them on, and do what I tell you. Then maybe you'll get a gold this time instead of choking."

Flecks of spit had hit her skin as he spoke, and she pointedly used the back of a hand to wipe them off.

"No."

"What did you say?"

"No. You know what? You're not my coach anymore," she said, blood rushing to her face.

"Stop being such a silly girl. Cool off, would you?"

She unfastened the belt, ripping it from her body. She scooped up the shoes and threw them as hard as she could until they slapped into the water, then followed them with the vest. He was watching her with his hands clenched into fists. His face was red, chest puffing.

"Get in there and fish those out right now! And put those shoes on like I told you."

She cut her eyes toward Tony, who stood next to his coach Phil. They were watching with wide eyes, and Tony was smirking like it was the best show he'd seen all year. She nodded to him then stomped away, answering Tim without looking back.

"Get them yourself!"

That night Hannah sat at the dining table with tears wetting her face, her head resting in the crook of an elbow. The adrenaline that coursed through her during the argument had left her depleted. Viv rubbed light circles on her back.

"What have I done?"

"It sounds like you didn't mean to do it, honey. You just lost your temper. Tim's lost his temper with you often enough! He should understand why it happened."

"I know, but he's not going to see it like that. He was furious!" she said, shaking her head into her arms.

"You've been under so much stress, Hannah. I hate to see you beating up on yourself like this. Why don't you sleep on it and call him in the morning?"

Her shoulders tightened, and she lifted her head. "What, and apologize to him?"

"If that's what you think you should do. I'm proud of you for standing up for yourself, but if you think you should have handled it differently, you could say so."

"I couldn't stomach that. No. I was going to talk to you about it tonight anyway. I was thinking of firing Tim already, but at the least, I would have had a short list of who could take over. The trials are only a month away! I'm screwed. I'll never find anyone to train me and get me up to where I need to be in that time."

"Hannah. You're an Olympic medalist. Surely you could find someone on short notice! Even if it was just to shore up everything you're already doing. And you're in peak form, you know exactly what to do. It'll work out; I'm sure of it. What about that guy that called a few months ago wanting to take over from Tim?"

"Who, Stuart Lanci? He's not a serious coach. I don't want to work with him."

"There will be somebody. We can start making calls first thing in the morning."

"Sure," Hannah said, taking a tissue from Viv's outstretched hand. "I'm exhausted. I'm going to take a bath and go to bed."

"Okay, sweetie."

In the tub Hannah stretched her legs, toes playing against the cold rim. The water was so hot it had stained her thighs red. More tears squeezed from the corners of her eyes, and she took a deep breath. Her mother was right. She'd been tense since she'd started preparing for Barcelona.

There was constant stress, piled on top of pressure. After the trials for Barcelona, there would be the Olympics. As soon as it was over, there would be a different event to fret over.

Though her family was only on the other side of this door, she felt so alone. Viv was so understanding, but she didn't quite get it, and she wished there was someone else to hash things out with. It took a few moments, but she realized it was Angie that she needed.

She hadn't allowed herself to think of Angie for a long time. She was crying harder now, and she dragged a washcloth over her face, so hard that it scratched against her skin.

Maybe she wouldn't think about Angie like this if she had a girlfriend. There hadn't been anyone at all since Angie, and so much of their relationship had been long-distance. It wasn't like she really knew what it was like to be with someone.

She was stunted, the oldest virgin in the world. Debbie and Marie had each had sex a long time ago. They made suggestions for her meeting a girl, but they weren't practical. She wasn't a student, so there was no gay campus group she could join. Her friends offered to go with her to one of the local gay bars, but when she imagined being recognized by strangers, it freaked her out too much.

When she got into bed, she pulled the sheet up and clutched it around her chin.

She was missing her life, chasing achievements that no longer meant much to her. The press following her around. The coach who treated her like shit. The inability to meet girls. The stress on her body, and the anxiety of never wanting to disappoint anyone. As she slipped into sleep, clarity was beginning to form with each deep breath.

CHAPTER EIGHTEEN

The next morning when Viv came to the kitchen, wearing a fuzzy robe with her hair sticking up, she was at the table going through her bank statements. As soon as the dawn sun slanted through her window, she had shot out of bed.

All night she'd dreamed anxiously about swimming, and the future had been settled in her sleep.

"What are you doing up? I thought you'd have your first sleep in for a while. Are you okay?" Viv said, resting a palm on Hannah's forehead.

"I am," she said, scribbling in a notebook she'd found on Paul's desk.

"What are you doing, honey?"

"Working out some stuff," she said, capping her pen. "Maybe get yourself a cup of coffee? I've got a few things to talk about."

Viv made them a mug each, putting one in front of her and sitting down across from her expectantly. "Okay, Hannah. I'm all ears."

"I'm quitting."

She repeated the phrase, trying to get used to it. Was she really going to throw everything away? The same thought must be passing through Viv's mind; she frowned with a hand on her chest. Though the fear made her feel like she was standing on a cliff's edge, she was light and free. She wanted to jump.

Viv took her hand. "Are you sure about this, Hannah? Maybe you just want to sit out Barcelona, get your bearings for a while?"

"I'm positive. I've been working out some financial stuff, how to get the most out of the money I've saved. Maybe put a deposit down on a place when I turn twenty-one. We talked about that. Mom, I'm just not happy anymore."

Tears stood out in Viv's eyes. Picking up her hand and putting it close by the notebook, she nodded firmly.

"That's all I need to know, sweetheart. You keep on going with this."

* * *

A week later she was at Marie's, hanging out in the middle of the day. She wondered if she'd ever get used to having this much free time. She'd been spending most of it here or with Viv, unwinding and trying to figure out her next move.

Marie's dorm room walls were plastered with posters of her favorite actors. Keanu Reeves, Christian Slater, Brad Pitt, and Val Kilmer pretending to be Jim Morrison, all smoldered down at Hannah.

The year before, Hannah and Marie watched *Thelma and Louise* until they could quote their favorite lines. After the third screening, she confessed that she preferred Geena Davis to Brad Pitt. It was the beginning of her coming out. Marie was shocked at first, but now she teases her about her crushes. Marie shamelessly pushed her toward any girl she thought might be remotely interested in women.

Marie was lolling on her unmade single bed with books spread around the bottom of the mattress. Rumpled clothes littered the carpet, and Hannah's nose crinkled at a musty smell.

"Has your mom seen this place? I feel like she'd be pretty mad if she saw what a hovel you've turned it into," Hannah said from the floor, where she sat cross-legged.

"Well yeah, she saw it when I first moved in, but she doesn't come over much. I go over there for family dinner. That's when we catch up."

"I still can't believe they're paying rent for you here when you live in the same city as them!"

"They wanted me to have the full university experience, which I am, by the way. I made out with the dude down the hall on Wednesday night. Not bad," she said, with a thumbs-up. "Eat your heart out, Scott."

"Good work. A-plus on this whole higher education thing."

Marie and Scott were on one of their frequent breaks, but Hannah guessed they'd get back together soon like they always did.

"Oh hey, have you seen the latest on your old friend Angie Thompson?"

The last big international event Hannah competed in before she retired was the Commonwealth Games in Auckland, and of course, as an American, Angie hadn't been there. She'd been waiting for Barcelona to see or hear any news about her.

"No. What happened?"

Marie sat up and rifled through the things at the end of her bed, then slapped a magazine down onto the carpet. "She got married. So young! She's like, only a year older than us."

"Huh," Hannah said. The magazine was thin and light; a weekly that Marie purchased for a few bucks to cut out pictures for her wall. The Kate Moss cover had a smaller image in the corner. A bride and groom, Angie in white.

She flipped quickly to the article. "America's Swimming Sweethearts." Angie's makeup was so thick it made her almost unrecognizable. Towering over her was Trent Baker, golden-haired and muscular. Hannah looked back and forth between their smiling faces, trying to figure out how Angie could fit with this plastic doll of a man.

She threw the magazine back, the pages fanning open as it hit the side of the bed and fell to the ground.

Marie rolled onto her side to look down at Hannah. "Why did you throw that?"

She clenched her jaw. If she ever got a girlfriend, no magazine would splash it across their pages unless it was to report on it as a scandal. Now Angie had what she'd always craved; the approval of the entire world. It didn't matter to Angie who she'd hurt to get it.

"What a pair of idiots. They're supposed to be training for the next Olympics, not having some stupid fairy tale wedding."

As soon as she called Angie that name, she felt bad about it. Having loyalty toward her was stupid, but she couldn't help it.

"I didn't think you'd be so cranky about it! Do you know him or something?"

"Nope. I mean, I know who he is. Hasn't been around as long as she or I have."

"I think he's a hottie."

"Sure."

"Are you all right? You're being weird. Are you mad that she didn't tell you? You were pretty close back in the day."

Hannah shrugged. She'd bitten her nails down to the quick, and she studied them, wondering why it was so hard to tell Marie about what had happened. Marie knew that Hannah liked girls now, so what was the big deal?

She stared at the wall behind Marie. "We were closer than I ever told you."

Marie shot up. "Holy shit! You've always said that you hadn't been with a girl yet? Tell me *everything*."

Marie's stunned expression made Hannah laugh, releasing tension she'd been holding for so long she didn't recognize herself. "It was nothing really, I guess. We never slept together or anything. I really liked her, though, and I thought she liked me too."

"Did you make out?"

"Sure. A lot, when she came over to visit."

"So, what happened? Wait...You did tell me she stopped writing to you, didn't you? But all you said was that she was self-centered or something?"

"That's all I ever knew. One minute we were full steam ahead and girlfriends and everything, and the next thing she didn't want to know me at all. We never broke up; she just started ignoring me. It was really hard."

She could tell Marie didn't know what to say, but the wheels of her mind were clearly turning. They'd been friends for a long time, and she knew Marie was dying to tell her that she shouldn't have kept this to herself. Marie lay on her side and patted the mattress.

"C'mon, come up here. I'm going to spoon you, and you can tell me more about it."

"No thanks!"

"Hannah. I don't care that you're a lemon. Get up here."

Nobody but her mom had hugged her since she'd been with Angie. She lay stiffly in her friend's arms, but it was nice to feel cared for like this. Once she started talking about Angie, she couldn't stop.

A month and many more tears later, she stood outside the entrance of The Diamond Hotel with Debbie and Marie at her side. It was a heritage-style building on the corner of two streets, in the northern part of the city.

There was nothing about the outside to indicate that it was one of the only lesbian bars in Melbourne.

"I can't go in, I don't want to. Let's just go down the street to somewhere else," Hannah pleaded.

Marie and Debbie each took an arm, trying to heave her forward.

"We've been talking about this since you had your retirement press conference! It's time to celebrate," Debbie said.

Hannah literally dug her heels into the ground. "We can celebrate somewhere else! C'mon, won't you two feel uncomfortable anyway?"

Marie took her by the shoulders. "Sweetheart. It's time you moved on. She's married. It's okay to have some fun now. All right?"

She nodded, screwing up her courage.

"Besides I want to get checked out by some lesbians. It will be super good for my self-esteem," Marie said. "Come in!"

A bouncer stepped out of the doorway into the streetlight, a tall woman with short, slicked-back gray hair. Her attention drifted back and forth between them. "Everything okay here, ladies?"

"Everything's fine. Thanks. We're just going to be on our way. Sorry to bother you," Hannah said.

Marie dropped Hannah's arm, sighing. The bouncer looked Hannah in the eye, moving closer. She had been slouching as she resisted her friends' pulling, but now she hauled herself up to full height.

"Go on in, sweetheart. You're welcome here, and everyone's very friendly. It'll get easier once you've been in the first time. Okay?"

Hannah looked at her friends, then walked forward.

As they approached the door, the woman held up a hand. "Wait a minute, are you all over age? I'm going to need to see some ID."

It was dim inside. Women were seated at stools at the bar, while others danced or played pool. The ends of cigarettes glowed brightly, moving through the air as they were raised up to mouths. Many faces turned toward Hannah and her friends as they entered, and she noted the appraising glances from a few women.

She raised her eyebrows at Marie and Debbie. She hadn't realized how much she'd enjoy being looked at like that again by other girls. "Shall we get drinks?"

"Yes please!" Debbie shrieked. "This is so fun!"

At the bar, Hannah looked past the woman wiping down the counter with a mat draped over her shoulder. On the other side, a girl stared back at her, someone who looked close to her age with a pixie cut and big brown eyes.

And she was cute.

They flirted silently while Hannah ordered a drink. When the bartender pushed a tall glass across to her, she wrapped a hand around it and nodded casually to her friends.

"Well, you'll have to excuse me, ladies. Talk amongst yourselves, I'm going to say hi to that girl."

CHAPTER NINETEEN

2000 - Melbourne

Hannah threw her arms over her head and checked her alarm clock. She almost bolted out of bed when she saw how late it was, but then it sank in that it was Sunday. Her rest day. It was the latest she'd slept in months. Angie hadn't left until after midnight.

Memories of the easy laughter they'd shared last night drifted through her mind. It made her smile, but a moment later her expression was blank again. Angie was gone now, and she wouldn't be eating dinner again with her tonight.

She rolled out of bed. Without Angie in it, her day seemed empty, though there was a family barbecue tonight at Viv and Paul's. They were having a small gathering for Mark and Ethan, who'd marked their birthday by going clubbing with friends the night before.

She caught up on her laundry and started clearing spoiled food from the fridge. When she was poking around in the shelves, she opened a container of leftover curry and fished out a chunk of tofu. Even cold, it was delicious, and she took out another piece. The phone was ringing, probably Viv calling to ask her to bring something tonight.

"Hey," Hannah said, still chewing.

"Hello?"

Hannah gripped the receiver with both hands. "Oh, hey, Angie! I was just eating some of that curry. So good."

"Oh yeah?"

Happy as she was to hear from her, she tried to figure out a polite way to ask why Angie might be calling.

"So, you're not going to believe this, but my flight got canceled!"

"Oh no! Can they get you on a later flight?"

"Well I tried, but it's just super expensive to change it, and the flights aren't at great times anyway. It's cheaper and easier to just check back in and pay for another night at the hotel, then fly out tomorrow. I was a bit frustrated, but honestly, it's all fine now. It's all worked out."

"Fair enough. I'm sorry to hear that. You won't miss anything important in Brisbane I hope?"

"It's a bit annoying, but no biggie. So, I don't want to impose or anything, but it leaves me free for dinner tonight. I could cook for you again if you'd want that?"

"Oh…"

Hannah bit her thumbnail. She couldn't miss her own brothers' birthday thing. Now she'd spend the whole night wishing she was somewhere else, with Angie. Before she could answer, Angie started talking again.

"Sorry, I *am* imposing, aren't I? I've been with you the last few nights! Forget I asked. Sorry. I'll let you go. I'll be fine. There are so many cool places around here to eat. I'll take myself out for dinner. I really don't mind at all. I could do with the rest anyway after such a late evening last night! Thanks again for everything. It was all super fun, and I had such a wonderful time. Anyway, I'll see you when you get up to Brisbane, okay?"

"No, wait!" Hannah said, laughing. It was hard to get a word in edgewise sometimes, but what might be annoying with someone else was only charming in Angie. "I'd love for you to come over, it's just that I'm going to my parents' place tonight. Mark and Ethan's birthday was on Friday. We're having a barbecue to celebrate."

"Right. Of course. Well. Tell your brothers I said happy birthday. Actually no, don't do that! They wouldn't remember me."

Hannah pushed a hand through her hair. She couldn't let Angie dine by herself, not after feeding her for the last couple of nights. "No, I'm sure they would remember you. Do you want to come with me? Nobody will mind an extra person, not at all. It's a casual thing."

"That's very generous, but you don't have to invite me."

"Be at my place at five. I'll drive us over."

Hannah hung up the phone before Angie could protest. She walked back to the fridge, thinking Angie wanted to come anyway. Hannah could hear it in her voice. She hummed to herself as she pulled wilted lettuce from the crisper to toss out.

Before thoughts could intrude that she'd be in the same position again tomorrow, wishing that Angie wasn't leaving the state, she told herself to look on the bright side. They had one more night to hang out. It was better than nothing.

At ten minutes to five, Angie knocked on the door, wearing the same blue dress she'd worn a couple of nights before. Her shoulders were finely sculpted, a work of art.

"I hope I'm dressed okay for tonight? Not a lot of choices. I only brought one case with me for the trip!"

"Are you kidding? You look gorgeous," Hannah replied, and Angie smiled back shyly at her. "I'll just grab my things, and we'll get going."

In the car, Angie drummed her fingers against the dashboard. Hannah watched from the corner of her eye, navigating toward her folks' place through the light Sunday traffic.

"You okay over there?"

"Does your whole family think I'm an asshole for what I did?" Angie asked, voice squeaking at the end.

"What do you mean? They don't know anything about anything. About you and me, I mean."

"You never told them?"

She took a hand from the steering wheel and found Angie's. It was only to calm Angie, because she still sounded so nervous.

"No, I didn't. Mom knew I was upset that we weren't talking, but she thought it was your usual regular teenage girl stuff. So, don't worry, okay? As far as they know, I'm just bringing an old friend to dinner. I called Viv today to tell her you were coming."

Angie threaded their fingers, tightening her hold for a moment. When Angie released her grip so Hannah could make a turn, the back of Hannah's knuckles grazed Angie's thigh.

She could feel Angie looking at her, so she willed herself to keep her eyes on the road.

They had been so well behaved the last couple of nights. They'd dined together and talked in the most civilized way, as though their kiss in the hotel pool had never happened.

Maybe it was a good thing Angie was going back to Brisbane the following day. Hannah wasn't sure how much longer she could keep this up.

It was dusk when they arrived at the house. She pulled up to the curb, the street crowded with Mark's van and Ethan's red Holden. She reached across to the glove compartment, carefully avoiding Angie when she popped it open. There were birthday cards for her brothers with gift vouchers for their favorite restaurant.

It was weeks since Hannah had been in the same place as her siblings, and she was looking forward to catching up with them. Angie paused, taking in the terrace house that stood unchanged save for a fresh coat of white paint on the exterior.

"Wow, this place. It's bizarre to see it again!"

She led Angie to the side gate. It creaked when she opened it for her, Angie brushing close by to pass her. There was the smell of cooking meat as they made their way down the narrow path toward the courtyard. Paul stood at the barbecue, egg flip in one hand and a bottle of beer in the other. His blond hair was thinning, and he'd developed a potbelly.

"Hey girls! Welcome. Everyone's still inside while I slave away out here. Would either of you like some beer?"

"I won't have one, thanks," Hannah replied. "But would you like one, Angie?"

"Sure, why not?"

"That's the way," Paul said, smiling broadly at her and leaning down to the cooler next to the barbecue. He pushed ice out of the way to fish out a bottle, then twisted off the top and handed it to Angie. "You're the American girl, aren't you?"

"One of them, sure!" Angie said.

"Haha...I remember you staying here. I always wondered how you two could get up and go to training so early like you did! Could always hear you giggling in the middle of the night and carrying on."

Paul looked down to flip burgers, and Hannah cut her eyes across to Angie, her eyebrows shooting up at the memory of why they made so much noise. Angie raised her eyebrows too.

Hannah guided Angie through the back door. A circle of people stood in the open-plan living and dining area. Viv was there, along with Mark and his wife, Jodie. Ethan and his girlfriend Belinda stood with their arms around one another.

Ethan and Mark still looked alike to Hannah, maintaining the exact same weight despite their very different lifestyles. They both had buzz cuts, and the easiest way to tell them apart was by Mark's scraggly mustache.

Though the brothers had chased after the same girls in high school, they'd ended up with partners who couldn't be more different. Jodie sported long blond hair parted down the middle. She wore strings of colored beads around her neck and always went braless. Belinda had dyed pink hair and a nose ring, and she dressed only in black. Hannah had never seen her without the thick black liner that swept up past the corners of her eyes.

"Ethan was so wasted he was falling all over the place," Mark said.

"Oh c'mon, I wasn't that bad. I lasted longer than you. You were practically passing out by the time we were at that last place."

"You both shouldn't drink so much," Hannah said, and everyone stopped talking.

"Hello sweetheart," Viv said, putting her arms out for a hug.

They pulled apart, Viv's eyes shining while she looked at Angie. Hannah put a hand on the small of Angie's back while she pointed and introduced each member of her family. "And this is Belinda, Ethan's girlfriend."

"So nice to meet you all," Angie said, hands clasped in front of her waist. "Well, and to see you again Mrs. Clark and Ethan and Mark, of course. It's been a long time."

"Viv! Even my kids call me Viv. It's great to have you here. If I remember correctly, you've had a family barbecue with us before, haven't you love?"

There was a subtle knowingness touching Viv's expression. She was suddenly sure her mother, always maddeningly perceptive, knew what Angie meant to her.

"Should we all move outside? I want to make sure Paul's not burning the sausages to a crisp like he always does," Mark said.

The night was unseasonably warm, and in the short time they'd been inside it had grown dark. Bamboo torches dotted the courtyard, and a Fleetwood Mac song played through the open kitchen window. They gathered around the outdoor table, passing plates and bowls across to one another.

Angie sat next to Belinda. Hannah listened to the contrast in the way they spoke, Angie sunny where Belinda's tone was flat and sarcastic. Against all the odds, they seemed to be getting along well.

When dinner was finished, Paul stood up from the table. "Everyone stay right here. I'm getting the cakes."

"I'll help," Viv said.

Paul loved to bake. Traditionally he produced two cakes for the boys, whom as children complained if they had to share. Viv and Paul disappeared inside, then carried out a sponge cake each, flickering candles lighting up their faces.

The group launched into "Happy Birthday." Hannah could make out Angie's voice, sweet and off-key in her ear. They sat so close to one another that their thighs touched under the table.

Her gaze lingered on Angie's profile, admiring the delicate point of her chin and her soft lips as she sang.

For the first time, she faced the fact that she was in deep waters. Having Angie here tonight was so right that she couldn't imagine what it would be like if she weren't. Jodie and Belinda had been part of their family for years, yet Angie clicked effortlessly into place beside them, completing the unit.

It was a crazy thought. They had reconnected so recently, and here she was, wanting Angie to be part of her family.

Yes, she was in very deep. So deep, that it might be called falling in love.

Reluctant to let the night slip from their grasps, Hannah and Angie outlasted the guests of honor. Mark and Jodie left at nine, Mark explaining that he was still recovering from his vicious hangover. An hour later Ethan and Belinda followed. Belinda asked for Angie's contact details before she said goodbye, which tickled Hannah.

When even Paul hid a yawn behind his hand, his nostrils flaring, Hannah said they should go.

"Do you mind if I use your phone to call a cab, please?" Angie asked Paul.

"Don't be silly! I'll drive you back to your hotel," Hannah said.

"Are you sure? It's pretty out of the way for you, isn't it?"

"It's fine! Thanks for dinner guys," Hannah said, kissing Viv's cheek. "I'll come around for dinner next Sunday?"

"Great. It was nice to see you, Angie. I hope I'll get to see you again sometime soon?"

Hannah shook her head at her mother's hopeful tone. Though she'd always tried her best with whomever Hannah brought home to meet her, it wasn't always the case for Viv to be this warm. She was quietly critical of Hannah's ex-girlfriends and hard to please.

They got into Hannah's car and she clipped her seat belt, glancing across at Angie before she put the key in the ignition. She hadn't said a word since they'd said goodbye to her parents.

"Everything good over there?" Hannah said, pulling out from the curb.

"Sure," Angie said, looking out the window.

"Did you have a nice time tonight? You and Belinda got along well."

"We did. Don't mind me. I'm just super tired. Thanks for driving me home, though."

Hannah pointed the car toward Angie's hotel, catching every red light on the way there.

It was going to be awkward to say goodbye when they'd already done it all the night before. And with Angie in such a weird mood, she didn't know what to say to her. She wished they could enjoy their last time together before Angie was leaving, and she hoped Angie was okay.

There was an open parking spot close to the hotel, and she pulled in, leaving the car running. "Well. I guess I'll be seeing you soon enough, huh?" she asked, breaking the silence.

Angie whipped around to face her. "I have to tell you something. I feel so bad. I can't keep it to myself anymore."

"Jesus, what?" What other secrets had she been hiding?

"I lied about the plane."

"What about the plane?"

"The...sorry!"

"Take a deep breath, and tell me what's going on," Hannah said, resting a palm on Angie's knee. Angie clutched her hand.

"I wanted to spend another night with you. My flight this morning didn't get canceled. I changed it. I figured I could fly back early tomorrow, and it wouldn't be a problem. When I got out of bed today, I just couldn't bear it, the thought of leaving, I mean. I should have been honest with you or just asked, instead of pushing myself into your family event like that. I thought we'd just have dinner at your place again and it wouldn't be a big deal. I never would have done it if I'd known you were going to feel so bad for me. I feel like I've pushed myself into your family gathering."

"Oh. Well. It's not a big deal, you were welcome, you saw that..."

Hannah began to giggle. Pretending to miss her plane was an over-the-top move on Angie's part, but it was adorable.

"Don't laugh at me!" Angie snapped, releasing Hannah's hand.

"I'm not! I mean, I know you like to cook, but…wow…" Hannah said, gasping for breath.

"I shouldn't have told you," Angie said. Her hands were folded in her lap, and she stared down at the floor. Hannah could see her profile in the near-dark.

She forced herself to stop, tapering off the giggles as she regained control. "Hey, no. Don't say that. Sorry. I'm just surprised is all. You have no idea how happy I was when you called."

"I was just having so much fun, and I wanted it to last a little bit longer. Gets lonely being in a new country and everything. So…You don't think I'm weird for what I did?"

"No. I think you're sweet. It's all okay. One hundred percent."

"Really?"

"Okay, maybe a little bit weird." A lopsided grin met her own. "Now come here and give me a big hug goodbye." She threw her arms open, folding Angie into an embrace. The gearshift dug into her thigh as she leaned over. Angie sank into her, and she tightened her hold.

It felt right to kiss the top of Angie's head, to show her how much she would miss her. Angie moved back and pressed her lips to Hannah's cheek, their silky softness light against her skin.

"Thanks for being so understanding," Angie whispered.

Hannah rubbed circles on Angie's back. The wings of Angie's shoulder blades were under her hand, Angie's breath brushing past her ear.

"I loved having you there tonight," Hannah said.

Angie kissed her cheek again, lingering so long this time that Hannah's stomach clenched. The desire was so great that there was no option but to turn her head and meet Angie's lips with her own.

It was immediate, the stoking of a fire that they were unable and unwilling to control. Angie kissed her deeply, until she was breathless.

Her lips were perfect for kissing. They were featherlight when they needed to be, full and passionate a moment later. She took Angie's bottom lip into her mouth, grazing her teeth against it.

What had they been doing all this time? All those wasted hours. No matter how much fun they'd been having, they should have been doing this.

Angie stroked Hannah's neck as they drank in one another. They crashed together like waves, moving in their seats.

Angie exhaled sharply. Not wanting to part, they pressed their lips against one another's again, Hannah trying to get her breath back.

Blood pounded in her ears. She glanced around the quiet street. Nobody was around.

"We're not supposed to be doing this, are we?" Angie asked.

"No," Hannah said, shaking her head.

When Angie moved closer and kissed Hannah once more, it was so tender it completely broke down the rest of her resistance. She liked Angie so much. What was she going to do with that?

She ran her hands up and down Angie's shoulders, feeling the fascinating combination of delicate bones, soft skin and hard muscle.

"Do you want to come upstairs?" Angie said, between kisses.

They leaned together with their foreheads pressed close. "I really, really want to. But like we just said…we're not supposed to, right?"

Angie moved back, but only a fraction. "What if we just continued making out?"

Hannah shrugged. "I mean, we're already doing that. A little privacy can't hurt."

"My thoughts exactly."

CHAPTER TWENTY

They gathered their purses and fled from the car, making their way through the hotel lobby, their shoes clicking along the marble floor.

In the elevator, Hannah stood close behind Angie. Even the ascent to Angie's floor was too long. Hannah checked around for a camera, and when none was visible, she pushed Angie's hair aside and dropped a kiss on the back of her neck. Angie backed into her, tilting her head to meet her mouth.

As the elevator dinged, they lurched through the opening doors, Angie scrambling for her keys. Finally, they were in the room, and they dropped their things, coming together urgently.

They kissed while Angie guided them toward the bedroom. When they arrived, they paused so they could slip off their shoes. They fell onto the bed together, Hannah sighing with relief that they were finally alone. Their tongues connected and they shared a deep kiss, lying on their sides.

Kissing Angie was the most sensual experience, filling Hannah with a toe-curling pleasure she couldn't remember having with anyone else. And when Angie rolled on top of her, so that her hair framed Hannah's face, it only got better.

Hannah leaned toward her as Angie focused all her attention on Hannah's lips. She raked her hands through Angie's hair, losing herself in its softness. It took a moment for her to realize Angie was moving to put a leg over her, to straddle her while they kissed.

Hannah ran her hands over Angie's back while Angie nipped at her mouth, alternating between kissing her softly and hungrily. Angie's legs were bent at the knee, and when Hannah slid her fingers over Angie's thighs, she realized how much her dress was riding up.

Hannah jerked her hands up, returning them to the plane of Angie's back. They were in dangerous waters, she knew that, and the further temptation was not going to help.

Angie pressed open-mouthed kisses to Hannah's neck, finding the sensitive places that made Hannah close her eyes and sigh. She gripped Angie's waist, moving her head back to expose more of her throat. Angie's tongue ran down the column of her neck, not stopping as she traveled further down. Hannah lightly gripped Angie's head in her hands as Angie kissed the flesh just above her cleavage.

Tentatively, as though waiting to see if Hannah was going to stop her, Angie slipped buttons from their eyes.

Hannah sat up so Angie could draw the shirt from her shoulders, and then Angie used her weight to push Hannah back down.

Angie flicked her tongue along the top of Hannah's breasts, and then she slipped down toward Hannah's abs. Hannah sucked in a breath when Angie's lips met her stomach. It was overwhelming, the sensation of Angie's mouth on her and Angie's silky hair trailing over her skin.

"God, I love your stomach..."

Hannah lifted her head to look at Angie but found she couldn't keep upright for long, so she lay back down. Angie shifted to kiss her, a palm slipping up and lightly over her breast. Hannah bit her lip.

"I mean. We could just agree to keep it above the waist, right?" Hannah managed to say.

Angie stared down at her, grasping her breast more firmly. She pulled the cups of Hannah's bra down roughly until Hannah moaned, her back arching when Angie's lips closed around a nipple, gently grazing it with her teeth. The ceiling fell out of focus as Angie caressed one breast and then the other.

This was moving fast, yet not nearly fast enough. Angie must feel the same; her mouth was on Hannah's again, kissing her hard, while her hands cupped and traced her breasts.

"This seems a little unfair," Hannah said, raising an eyebrow. Angie frowned, but then the meaning sunk in.

Angie unzipped her dress and pulled it over her head. Hannah hadn't even thought about the fact that, clearly, she couldn't be topless without taking the whole thing off.

Hannah's hands returned to Angie's hips. Her gaze trailed over the beautiful expanse of her stomach, her fine collarbones, and the swell of her breasts in a light blue bra. Dipping a little lower, she saw that Angie wore matching underwear, a hint of lace on their upper edge.

Angie reached back to undo her bra, and their eyes locked as she dragged it down her arms, then threw it onto the floor. Hannah gripped her by the hips. The shape of her was breathtaking. After a moment she flipped Angie onto her back, each of them laughing as Angie wrapped her legs around Hannah's waist.

Hannah traveled downward, tasting Angie's skin, reveling in the way Angie writhed underneath her. She teased her tongue over Angie's breasts so that Angie's breath was loud in her ear.

Angie reached for the button of Hannah's jeans, halting the kiss. "Is this okay? Just evening things up, right? If I'm only in my underwear…" Angie said raggedly.

"Oh, of course, you're absolutely right," Hannah said, helping Angie tug her jeans over her hips. Hannah unhooked the bra that was still wrapped awkwardly around her waist, throwing it on the floor as Angie had done.

With nothing but thin layers of cloth between them, the friction between them grew even sweeter.

Angie wedged her leg between Hannah's thighs and they strained against one another. It struck Hannah as funny that they were acting like the horny teenagers they'd been once upon a time, dry humping on the bed like this. Before she knew it, she was giggling into Angie's mouth.

Angie looked up at her.

"Nothing. I don't know."

Angie placed a hand on either side of her head. "You might like to try and explain what's so damn funny! Laughing at a time like this?"

"It's nervous laughter! Nothing. Sorry," she said hopelessly.

Angie shook her head, pulling Hannah down. They were pushing into one another more earnestly now, kissing furiously. Angie rolled on top of her, lying on her side and raking her eyes over Hannah's breasts once more.

Then her mouth was everywhere, licking and kissing her breasts, working dangerously low on Hannah's stomach. Nothing like it had ever happened before, but Hannah was beginning to consider that it wouldn't be so crazy for her to orgasm without Angie even touching her below the waist.

When Angie shifted up this time, they kissed slowly, Angie's hand was measured as it rubbed over her breasts, then outlined the angle of her hip. When Angie's palm firmly grasped her thigh, Hannah groaned.

"Maybe we should stop," Hannah said.

"Why, don't you like it?" Angie teased, fingers fluttering over her stomach now. Hannah grabbed her hand, and Angie froze, her eyes wide. "I'm so sorry!"

"No, don't worry," Hannah said in a rush, taking Angie's hand and kissing it. "I like everything you do. Trust me. It's just that I'm kind of a little worked up here. That's all."

"You are?"

Hannah nodded. "Aren't you?"

"Of course, I am." When she whispered in Hannah's ear, her hot breath raised gooseflesh on Hannah's arms. "You make me so wet. I wish I could feel how wet you are."

Hannah swallowed hard. She hadn't expected dirty talk like that from Angie, but she liked it. A lot.

They should talk about it more than this, Hannah knew that, but right now she didn't care. They were adults, and they could do whatever they wanted.

And oh, how she wanted.

"You can. If you really mean that," Hannah said with her arms around Angie's neck, staring into green eyes that flooded with heat when she spoke.

Without looking away, Angie reached down between them. Her palm lay flat on Hannah's stomach and then she edged it into Hannah's underwear. Hannah closed her eyes, her mouth dropping open at the way Angie touched her, fingers sure and adoring.

Angie paused to strip off Hannah's underwear and then her own, the garments joining their bras on the floor. While Angie was busy throwing their things aside, Hannah had the first moment of self-consciousness since they'd started.

The air was fresh on her bare skin, then Angie twisted toward her. "Hey. Are you okay?"

"Yes," Hannah replied.

"Do you want me to turn the light off?"

"I'm all right with having it on if you are."

Angie gathered Hannah in her arms to hold her, kissing her softly and brushing her hair from her face.

Hannah rolled her eyes, more at herself than anything. Jesus, Angie wasn't just incredibly sexy in bed, she was also very considerate and warm. And they hadn't even done the deed yet! She hated to think how far gone she was going to be when they did.

"I don't want to do this if you're not sure about it," Angie said, looking into her eyes. "I like just being near you, like this."

In the background, the air-conditioning unit clicked, and a car horn sounded from outside. But they were safe in here, alone and far away from prying eyes.

"I'm not even a little bit unsure," Hannah said.

She put her arms around Angie's neck again, and they joined in a searing kiss that swept the tenderness of the last moments away. She tilted her hips to indicate that she was ready, and Angie slid her hand down her stomach again, Hannah's eyes fluttering shut.

It was as good as she'd known it would be, Angie watching her face and kissing her as she touched. Angie knew just when to speed up, not at all afraid to ask Hannah what she liked and how she wanted it.

Soon Angie was inside her, her thumb still stimulating Hannah in the most beautiful way. Hannah loved being able to feel the warmth of Angie's form pressed down against her. Their skin was slick as the heat rose between them, their hips moving together.

Hannah put her hands across Angie's back, splaying her fingers out so that she could feel shifting muscles beneath firm skin. The rhythm of Angie's movements drummed against her until Hannah's entire body clenched. She looked up into green eyes in the same moment that Angie curled her fingers and the sensation tore through her.

Hannah had never been a particularly loud person in bed, but when she called out Angie's name, she was shocked at how her voice echoed in the room.

A moment later she threw her arm across her face. "Sorry. I didn't mean to yell like that."

Angie's eyes sparkled. "Don't be embarrassed. That's not really the kind of thing you need to apologize for."

"Okay," she said. Angie was still cupping her between her legs, and when she pressed her hand briefly, Hannah gasped.

Angie kissed her delicately, the heat already building between them again. "I'm so glad I have tonight with you. I've wanted you for so long."

"So have I," Hannah said. "And we've got all night. Who needs sleep?"

"Not me," Angie replied as Hannah rolled on top of her. "We've got an awful lot of lost time to make up for."

CHAPTER TWENTY-ONE

In the morning Hannah reclined in the rumpled bedclothes, resting while Angie was in the shower. The sound was muffled by the half-closed door and the fan, but Angie was singing in her off-key way. It was adorable.

Hannah couldn't quite fathom that this had happened, nor could she believe *how* it had happened. They'd agreed to be only friends, but she didn't regret it, not even a tiny bit. And judging by the fact that Angie had woken her up to make love yet again an hour ago, there was no regret on Angie's part either.

A cloud of steam followed Angie out of the bathroom. A plush white towel was wrapped around her, another towel curled tightly around her hair like a turban. Angie walked over to the bed to kiss Hannah, and then she threw open the closet door to rifle through hangers.

"I should really get it together and pack, but it's not easy to focus with you lying there in your birthday suit," Angie said. She gathered up underwear and clothes and went back to the bathroom.

"I'm sooo sorry," Hannah called out. "What time's your flight?"

"Eleven. How long do you think it'll take me in the cab this time of day? Is forty-five minutes long enough?"

"You're not getting a cab. I'll drive you."

"That's sweet of you, but don't you have things to do?"

"I already told Neil I was sick, and I couldn't go to training this afternoon even if I wanted to!"

In the early hours, when they were dozing, Hannah gathered the presence of mind to leave a message for Neil saying that she wouldn't be meeting him today. It was a long time since she'd called in sick. Though she wasn't used to blowing off training, one day hardly mattered.

"I'll take it, thank you. I'm sure you're much better looking than the taxi driver would have been."

Hannah laughed, sitting up in bed with the silky sheets tucked around her. She should get out of bed and put on some clothes, but she didn't want to move. All she wanted to do was watch Angie.

Angie emerged from of the bathroom again, in her white dress. Hannah watched the sway of her hips as she crossed the room to pick up the phone.

"What are you doing?"

"I'm ordering us room service! We need to have breakfast."

Hannah eyed Angie's legs as she ordered pastries, fruit, juice, and coffee. Now that she thought about it, she was ravenous.

When Angie hung up, she lay down on top of the sheet with her head on Hannah's chest. "Just for a minute, until the food comes, and then I really will pack."

"Are you trying to miss your flight again? Was it that good?"

Angie nuzzled closer. "Don't flatter yourself."

They held hands. Hannah realized they could stay in this space with the kissing and the fun banter until Angie was gone, but she couldn't let her go without at least trying to talk about all of this. Yet she struggled to find the right words.

"I know we kept saying we weren't supposed to…but I just wanted to say that I'm happy about last night," Hannah said.

Angie looked up at her. "Me too. When we were younger, I wanted you to be my first, you know? I was always sad that it never happened like that, and angry about it too, but now it doesn't seem to matter so much. Now it feels like things have gone exactly the way they were supposed to."

The words stopped Hannah's heart. They captured precisely how she felt, though she would never have Angie's courage. She could never have said those words first.

"Sorry, was that too much?" Angie said.

She stroked thick hair, sifting it through her fingers. "Not at all. I was thinking that you were right. I wished for that too."

"So...where to from here?" Angie said.

Was it crazy that Hannah wanted to say, "To hell with everything. Let's give this a try?" Stupid, because there were so many obstacles. Their locations, the fact that Hannah was in the middle of preparing for the Games, the reality that Angie was one of her coaches.

There was no way this could work.

"I don't know, Angie. I know that I really like you. But it's complicated, isn't it? It seems kind of impossible right now. Tell me what you think."

Angie sat up to meet Hannah face-to-face, her green eyes a mixture of emotions Hannah found hard to pin down. There was worry there, and sadness. Angie put a hand to the side of Hannah's face.

"I like you too, but I guess I'm worried about the very same things you must be. I know how important these Games are to you. I know how much work there is ahead of you. I could never forgive myself if I distracted you in any way, or if the team found out about us, and it did anything to your reputation. And of course, I don't even live here! I'll most likely be going back to the States soon, and if we start anything, it'll just make that harder. So, as much as I wish things were different, I know that we have to take all that stuff into account."

They stared at one another, solemnly. It would do no good to pretend that it was any other way.

Hannah took Angie's hand and kissed her palm. "The Games aren't so far away, you know. And I don't even know how much longer I'll be swimming after that. I'm a little too old to think that there will be much beyond Sydney. The whole point of coming out of retirement was to do another Games."

Eyes welling up, Angie drew her hand away. "Listen. The Games are the most important thing right now. I want you to get the gold. This is about you. You should already have one."

"It's not about settling old scores. It's nothing like that."

"I know, but you should have beat me. That killed me. I didn't even want to look at my gold medal for a few years to be honest with you. This time, I don't want to have anything to do with your performance outside of my job as coach."

"So what do we do about all of this?"

"We could just take a pause, right? We could wait until the Games are over, then reassess. It will still be hard then, with me going back to the States, but at least we'll have space and time to work things out without the Games complicating everything."

"A pause. I like that idea," Hannah said. "I mean, I don't. But you know what I mean. It's a solution."

Angie put a hand behind her head, grabbing a bruising kiss. When they broke for air, Hannah licked her lower lip. Even after the long hours of being together, they weren't close to spending their passion.

"That's the last time, okay?" Angie said.

"For a while."

"Only for a while."

CHAPTER TWENTY-TWO

The pause came with rules. They may have been necessary, but Hannah soon hated them. Hannah and Angie had agreed that until the Games were over, there would be no contact between them unless it was professional.

"How do I know you're even going to be still into me when the Games are over?" Hannah asked in the car on the way to the airport, hiding her sharp fear under a light tone.

Angie scoffed. She put her hand high on Hannah's leg. "Do you seriously think that's a real risk? I'm still into you after ten years, remember?"

Now Hannah tried to hold fast to those words each time she thought of Angie. A thousand times a day, she told herself that she could be sure Angie's attraction wouldn't wane in a few short months.

Tonight, she was having dinner with Marie, and she was grateful for the company. The week had been a grueling one, with more commitments than she'd wanted. A reporter and camera crew from Channel Six news interviewed her poolside one morning at training, and there was a big endorsement meeting the following day. It didn't help that she began the week very sleep deprived, though she was hardly going to complain about that given the cause.

When Marie burst through the door with a brown paper bag full of junk food, Hannah cracked the first real smile that had crossed her face in days.

They set themselves up at the dining table. Marie had picked burgers up from Archie's, a burger joint owned by two brothers just down the street from Hannah's place. In her role as a restaurant consultant, Marie had helped put Archie's together and the brothers still gave Marie a discount every time she went in.

Marie put a handful of fries on her burger, squashed the bun down with two hands, then cut it in half. Hannah observed the familiar ritual before attacking her own burger.

"How's Scott? You said things weren't going great at work last time we talked about him?"

"Yep. His boss was being a jerk, but they had a man-to-man talk over a beer or some shit and worked everything out," Marie said, rising to open the pantry. Marie's faded sweatpants had a baggy seat. She couldn't tease her, not when she was sporting equally worn sweats and an old gray T-shirt riddled with holes.

Marie returned to the table with a bottle of hot sauce, pouring it over her fries.

"Glad to hear things are okay."

"Oh! Oh, I just remembered, Angie was coming over last time I was here. You flaked out on calling me again. How was it?"

"It was good, good."

Marie put her burger down. "Why are you blushing?"

"I'm not. We hung out, and then her flight back got delayed."

"And? *And?*"

Who was she kidding? She wanted to tell Marie. She'd been dying to talk about this. "I invited her to Mark and Ethan's birthday dinner. Then we went back to her hotel and..."

Marie raised her eyebrows. "You slept together? Wow, and you didn't call me? Now I know where I stand!"

"Sorry. I guess I feel a bit weird about it. Obviously, it wasn't supposed to happen. Angie's going to be my coach. She lives in Brisbane for now, but she'll go back to America after all this. And so on."

"Sounds like there are some obstacles, sure, but where did you leave it?"

She sighed. "We agreed that we'd wait and maybe pick things up again after the Games. Just see how things go. But it's hard to imagine a solution to all this when she lives in another country most of the time. We'll see. I know that I'm very interested and so is she."

Marie took the last bite of her burger, chewing slowly. "Hmm."

"Hmm, what? Do you have something you'd like to say?"

"Do you remember when Scott and I broke up for a while? After we'd gotten serious, I mean, when I was about twenty?"

How could she forget? At first, Marie was heartbroken by the split. Hannah was a shoulder to cry on throughout long nights of drinking, Marie rattling off all the ways Scott had hurt her. Soon afterward, she started dating a few different guys in quick succession.

"I went out with that German dude with the heavy accent. He lived in Perth? Michael."

"I do remember him, yeah," Hannah said. There was a picture in her mind of a lanky boy with a blond-haired goatee. Michael played the guitar and smoked rolled cigarettes. They'd all hung out together one night in Marie's dorm room, drinking boxed wine.

"I thought he was my dream man. Super good-looking, seemed really mature compared to Scott. A little older, had a good job in finance...I spent three weeks with him while he was visiting friends over here."

"Marie. I just said I remember him. What's the point of this story?"

"I thought we were crazy about one another. I was thinking long-term, already had us married in my mind. I was ready to forget all about Scott."

There was no point in pressing her about getting to the point. Marie pushed her plate away and leaned back in her chair, one leg crossed over the other. Hannah resisted the urge to get up and clean up the table. Marie loved to talk, and after all, she had just brought her dinner.

She gestured for her to go on.

"He went back to Perth, but of course, we'd promised to stay in touch. We talked on the phone all the time, sent letters back and forth. I saved my money so I could go and see him."

The ending of the story was clearing for Hannah, the fog in her memory floating away. It wasn't so long ago. She'd been there to comfort Marie when she'd arrived home, deflated.

"Then when I went to see him, there was nothing there. I met holiday Michael, but when he was in his own city and his own home, he was inconsiderate. Acted like I was in his way unless we were having sex at the time. I left Perth wondering why he'd bothered to keep in touch. And when I got back, I never spoke to him again."

"And then Scott came to see you, and he'd made all those changes. You and Scott got back together and lived happily ever after. So?"

"I hope things work out with you and Angie, I do. But I just want you to remember that you don't really know this girl."

"I'm aware," Hannah said. She rose and scrunched up the waxed paper that the burgers had been wrapped in and carried their plates to the sink.

"I'm just trying to be a good friend, Hannah. I don't want you to get hurt. She screwed everything up for you once already."

She twisted around. "We're not sixteen anymore! I hardly think she's going to disappear on me again now. And it's not so long ago that you were acting like she'd probably changed by now. Remember that?"

"I do, but I meant you should give her a chance as friends and colleagues. It's not just about that," Marie said gently.

"You're really gone on her, I can tell. I'm happy that you've found someone you like this much because I've never seen you like this before. That also means I'm a little scared for you. It would be so easy to confuse what you felt back then, that first love high, with what's going on now. That's all I'm saying."

She looked back at Marie for a beat, crossing her arms. If she were honest with herself, she could admit that for those precious few days she and Angie lived in a bubble. They had shrouded themselves in fantasy, pretending that it wasn't just for a while. They'd talked about it, acted like they were being realistic. But at the same time, they might have no future.

If she were going to be able to truly focus on the Games, Hannah would need to stop daydreaming about Angie and about the life they could make together. This might lead to nothing, just as Marie was trying to tell her.

She folded Marie into a hug. "Okay, I've heard you. Don't worry about me, I'll keep myself in check."

For the next week, Hannah held firm to that promise. She drove thoughts of Angie from her mind and recommitted herself to training. The water glided past her muscles. At the gym, she took pleasure in dripping sweat, the evidence of how hard she was working.

On Sunday afternoon she drove to her folks' place, thinking that seeing her mom would be an excellent distraction. Hannah let herself in, finding Viv in the courtyard sprawled on a lawn chair with a copy of *The Age* and a glass of wine.

"Hello sweetheart," Viv said, folding the broadsheet in half and putting it aside. The aviator sunglasses she wore were Paul's, and despite the lateness she was still in her polka-dot nightgown. It was nice to see her relaxing since she'd always been the kind of person who did ten things at once.

She kissed Viv hello then reclined in the chair next to her. A neighbor's tree hung over the fence, the branches swaying against the clear blue sky.

"You look like you're having a nice afternoon out here. Where's Paul?"

"Visiting your grandmother. He went over there for lunch. I had the most refreshing sleep in this morning, haven't slept that late in years. So. You're alone this time?"

"What do you mean? Why wouldn't I be?"

"I can't think why…oh, that's right! You brought a friend with you last time you were here if I recall."

Hannah grabbed Viv's wineglass and took a sip. "Ugh, you're drinking the cheap stuff? And you knew Angie was flying back the next day."

"I was just looking for a way to bring up that I think Angie is a *lovely* girl. And don't be a snob. I happen to like this wine."

"Angie's very nice. I agree."

Viv squinted at her. "I'm your mother, Hannah."

"What are you getting at?"

"You know very well what I'm getting at. I see things. The way she looked at you!" Viv said, fanning herself with a hand. "I thought I was going to have to call the fire department."

"Stop teasing."

"I'm just saying, she was looking at you like Meg Ryan looked at Tom Hanks in *Sleepless in Seattle*. Like you hung the moon."

"Oh, please. That's the worst comparison I've ever heard, and you know I hate those movies. Can we talk about something else? Tell me about work."

"Now I know you're hiding something. You never want to hear about that!"

After they'd talked for a while, she settled back into the chair while her mother picked up the newspaper again.

"Oh hey, look, speak of the devil! Here's your friend," Viv said, angling the sports section toward her.

Angie was standing poolside with a swimmer, one of the Brisbane women who was a frontrunner in the butterfly stroke. It was yet another story about the American defecting to Australia. Angie's hand was on the swimmer's shoulder, and they leaned close together.

On the drive home, Hannah twisted the dial to turn the music up, trying to shift her focus away from Angie. She knew she was being ridiculous, but she couldn't stop thinking about Angie up there in Brisbane, spending time with other women. Why had she decided to trust her again so quickly? She'd never been the jealous type but maybe Marie had a point. They didn't know one another that well.

Ricky Martin's cheesy pop could only take her so far, and when she couldn't find anything else but talkback radio, she clicked the radio off with a sigh.

Everyone had an opinion about her relationship with Angie. As time went on and people like Viv and Marie got it out of their system, all this discussion would end. At least she hoped so. It might mean that her own thoughts would turn to Angie less often.

In her apartment she rolled up the blind at the backdoor so she would have enough light then swept, picking up the loads of dust that collected no matter how often she cleaned.

She was working through a pile of laundry when she decided she should check her email. She hadn't looked at it since Angie was there, and she was trying to get into the habit of replying to anything business related. She listened to the screech of the modem dialing, mindlessly clicking the mouse button until the Internet connected.

Angie Thompson. The time stamp told her that the email had been flung through cyberspace in the early hours of Saturday morning.

The message was simple. *I've been thinking about you.*

How could one line convey so much and come across as that suggestive?

They couldn't do this. This email was most likely thanks to a moment of weakness for Angie. Over the past two weeks, Hannah had been tempted to break the rules more than once herself.

The kindest thing to do was to let it go. It was the best thing for both of them. She pushed her chair back from the desk and walked away.

CHAPTER TWENTY-THREE

2000 - Brisbane

Stuart Lanci's home matched his personality, calling attention to itself in every way. Many of its surfaces were reflective—marble benches and mirrored tiles. The black and gray fabric of the drapes and furniture coverings were accented by pops of color, from red ornaments and abstract canvases.

In the dining room, large chairs with soft black seats were drawn up to the oak table. Alongside serving platters, there were red roses in gray ceramic vases. Stuart's wife Kasey had served the team a low-fat feast of chicken breasts, greens, and a grain salad.

Angie was seated diagonally across from Hannah, at Stuart's right hand. When she lifted her water glass, it trembled slightly in her grip.

Stuart tapped the side of his glass with a spoon, making a chiming sound that silenced the guests.

Pushing back his chair, Stuart stood with his chest puffed out. His blue-eyed gaze alighted on each team member, holding eye contact for a moment before moving on to the next.

He looked the part of the aging playboy with silver hair shaped by an expensive cut and healthy glowing skin. He wore neatly pressed slacks with a royal blue linen shirt.

The Lancis were one of the wealthiest families in Melbourne. There were whispers that he didn't have what it took to achieve success in his own right. With piles of inherited money, he didn't have to work, and it shocked everyone when he got involved in swimming.

At first the sporting community took it for a foolish hobby and Hannah hadn't taken him seriously. But in the past ten years, his medal count had outstripped more experienced coaches, and now he was respected. He'd never mentioned that Hannah had rejected him as a coach when she was younger, but it hung between them sometimes.

"Thank you all for being here today. This is the beginning of a momentous journey. The next few weeks we're going to work you very hard, but I know that all of you are more than up to the challenge. With the help of my assistant coaches, Angie and Jack here, we're going to get this team tight," he said, holding up a clenched fist.

There were murmurs of agreement, and he rounded the table with his eyes again, pinning his audience in place.

"You're all extraordinary swimmers or you wouldn't be here. But winning takes more than that. For us to attain results we can all be proud of, it's going to take heart and guts. These are the Sydney Games, my friends. These are *our* Games. The whole country is going to watch us forge history. You can't just be great swimmers as individuals; you're a team. And then, you are all vital parts of a larger team, standing shoulder to shoulder with the athletes of every stripe representing this great nation."

Hannah wondered whether this speech was rehearsed and sought out Angie's eye. He was orating like a holy rolling preacher at a revival meeting. Though her expression betrayed nothing, Hannah was sure she was beating back laughter too.

Hannah winked. She almost felt bad when Angie covered a chuckle with a cough. When his attention wandered toward her, Angie took a gulp of water.

"Excuse me," Angie said.

"That's all right. This night, us breaking bread together, is a symbol of our commitment to one another. Nothing's more important than protecting one another, supporting your teammates as though they're your family. And it goes without saying that I don't want to hear about any funny business. Nothing that will bring disrepute to the team. But anyway, enough of all that. For the rest of the night, get to know your peers. Enjoy yourselves. *Mingle*. Here's to Australia!"

He held up his tumbler of whiskey, and each guest raised their glass of iced mineral water.

The team members drifted away from the table, filling the adjoining living room with the buzz of conversation. Rachel Willis stood alone in the corner, facing bookshelves. Hannah tapped her on the shoulder, and Rachel turned, smiling hopefully.

"How are you doing, Rachel?"

"This is all pretty overwhelming!"

"I know. It's still scary for me, and I've done this before."

Rachel twirled hair around a finger. "Really? You seem so relaxed."

From behind Rachel, Hannah could see Angie in her black shift dress talking to Stuart. Her hair was knotted into a messy bun, exposing the soft skin of her neck. When Angie looked at her and stopped talking for a moment, Hannah quickly pulled her focus back to Rachel, touching her shoulder.

"It's a lot. It's normal to feel nervous. I just want to let you know you can talk to me anytime if you have any questions or just want to vent. Okay?"

"Thank you so much, Hannah, I really appreciate it."

"No worries." Angie was alone now, eyes darting around as though she was looking for someone to talk to. "Excuse me, I'm going to say hi to someone on the coaching team."

"Hello," Angie said, biting her lip and scanning Hannah's form up and down. "You look good."

"You don't look so bad yourself."

"How are you feeling? Are you ready to work hard in training?"

She couldn't resist getting closer to whisper, taking in the scent of Angie's perfume. She loved the thought of Angie getting ready for tonight, knowing they would see one another. Angie might have thought of her when she was spraying it on, knowing how much Hannah liked it.

"What are you going to do to me if I'm not?"

Angie flushed. "Well. I'm glad you don't seem to be upset with me."

"Why would I..."

"Hey, Jack!" Angie said, blinking rapidly.

Hannah angled her body to let Jack into the conversation. The assistant coach was the same height as Angie, and he had the stocky, muscular build of a wrestler. Hannah liked him immediately. His brown eyes were warm and gentle.

"Hi, there! I'm a big fan," Jack said, sticking out an arm to shake Hannah's hand.

"That's nice of you to say. It's great to meet you."

As she chatted with Jack, Stuart approached to talk to Angie. With her peripheral vision, she watched as Angie was whisked away. This night was crucial for team building, but she hadn't prepared herself for how difficult it was to see Angie amongst this sea of people.

She wanted more than anything for them to be alone. Still, when getting to know her teammates, she had to bring the same enthusiasm that she would to a training session. As one of the senior members of the team, it was her responsibility to set a good example. Working the room, she divided her time as evenly as she could.

Rachel was gushing about the football-playing boy she'd recently started dating, when Hannah clocked Angie standing in the doorframe by herself, watching her with those glittering green eyes. When their gazes snagged, Angie tilted her head toward the side, signaling for Hannah to come to her.

"It's so great to date a fellow athlete, you know? He wants to do it professionally, so he gets how important all this stuff is," Rachel said.

"That's wonderful, Rachel. Can you excuse me for a second?"

Hannah slipped past the guests and down the hall to where Angie waited in a doorway. She stepped back inside as Hannah got closer, and soon they were in Stuart's study. Hannah softly pushed the door shut behind them.

Floor-to-ceiling shelves housed books, magazines, glass paperweights, and silver-framed photos. The study was otherwise sparsely furnished. A large black desk stood in the middle of the room, a matching black chair arranged in front of it.

"I would never have imagined Stuart owning so many books," Hannah said, running her finger along a row of spines. "Do you think he hired someone to pick them all out for him?"

Angie leaned against the desk with her arms crossed over her waist. At Hannah's joke, she let out a small laugh, looking down at the carpet.

Hannah sobered, treading closer to her. "I gather you got me in here to talk. What did you mean before? You said something about me being upset with you?"

"Sorry. I didn't mean to be dramatic or anything. I wanted to apologize for breaking the rules with that email. You were training and I have no excuse."

"Of course, I'm not upset with you! I thought it was best that I didn't reply. I knew what it might lead to."

"I know."

Why hadn't she sent a quick note in return, so Angie would know everything was okay? Was there an ugly hidden part of her that wished to pay Angie back?

Drawing still nearer to Angie, she searched herself and knew that it wasn't the case. When she was close, she heard the pace of Angie's breath quicken. A wisp of hair had loosened from Angie's bun. She pushed it behind her ear and then trailed a finger along the side of her face, ending on the gentle slope of her chin.

"What are you doing?" Angie said, finally meeting her gaze.

Hannah cupped her face, her thumb tracing Angie's full lips. "You know. Do you want me to stop?"

"Hey, that's my line!"

Hannah glanced over her shoulder to make sure the door was closed.

Hurriedly, she pressed her lips to Angie's, tasting their sweetness. Angie sighed against her mouth, shifting her hands to Hannah's waist.

At first, Hannah was careful to hold her body still and to stay back. The restraint lasted only for an instant. Overcome by having Angie like this again, Hannah kissed her fiercely and was kissed fiercely in return.

When Angie's tongue slid into her mouth, Hannah pushed more firmly against her. She lifted Angie onto the desk, so that soon she was curling her legs around Hannah's waist.

Angie pushed her hand into Hannah's hair at the back of her head, scratching lightly at her scalp. They broke off breathlessly, smiling at one another.

"I'm not sure this is what Stuart meant when he said we should mingle," Hannah said.

"Maybe not. It might even qualify as funny business. But personally, I'm in favor," Angie said.

She laid a kiss on one of Angie's cheeks, then the other, finally touching her mouth to Angie's temple. "I missed you."

"I missed you too."

They looked into one another's eyes, Hannah drawing comfort from the care in Angie's. Then, she put her arms around her, holding her firmly, loving the way Angie burrowed her head into her shoulder. It was quiet, just the two of them breathing against one another.

"We really shouldn't be doing this," Hannah said.

"I know."

"So this was really the last time."

"I know."

Hannah's eyes drifted shut, and she let herself go. She forgot where they were, only feeling safe and warm. Despite her calm, her heart was beating like a drum.

Angie started. There were voices from the hall, a couple of the swimmers searching for the bathroom.

"We should get back out there, I guess," Hannah whispered. She kissed Angie's temple once more, hair brushing against her lips. Next time they saw one another, it would be at training, and Hannah would have to deal with the frustration of having so many people around again.

"You're right. You go first, and I'll follow you soon, okay?" Angie said.

Hannah stood in front of Angie, taking both Angie's hands in her own.

There were so many things she wanted to say, like she was starting to think that she couldn't go back from this feeling. After this was all over, she wanted everything Angie had to give. She wanted to say that this was anything but just a fling for her.

When Angie squeezed her hand, Hannah could swear that somehow Angie knew exactly what she was thinking.

Stealing one more kiss, she moved back, their hands joined for as long as they could before they parted.

CHAPTER TWENTY-FOUR

The relay team lined up beside the pool, the four of them in their bathers and caps, goggles snapped into place. In her green and gold polo shirt, Angie clutched a sheaf of papers. Below the hem of her black shorts, her toned legs drew Hannah's eye.

It was hard not to stare, now that she knew how Angie shivered at a touch on her inner thigh. On her knee was a pink scar from a childhood cycling accident, and she painted her toenails because she hated the way they looked bare.

When Hannah looked up, she realized that Angie had clocked what she was doing. Hannah promised herself she wouldn't do it again. Angie deserved more, even if there was a glint in Angie's eye that hinted that she wasn't bothered by Hannah's ogling.

At Hannah's side stood Rachel Willis. Meghan Jeffries and Andrea Honeysett rounded out the group. Though Hannah didn't know either of them well, they were each impressive. Andrea had taken a bronze medal at the last Olympics in Atlanta. It was a team Hannah was proud to be a part of.

Clearing her throat, Angie held the papers at her side. When she spoke, her voice was full of confidence.

"As a coaching team, we acknowledge that you're all in peak form and that each of you has individual coaches with whom you've worked hard. This part of the training is only about developing cohesion. We're here to make sure that we've got the sequencing right. We've taken a look at your most recent recorded times, and we'll be trying out the following order. Rachel first, then Andrea, followed by Meghan. Hannah will be anchor."

Hannah dipped her head along with the rest of the team. The order was predictable. Though Hannah had bested Rachel in the trials, Rachel's times were consistently faster than hers. It made sense that Rachel should lead.

The team split in half to position themselves at opposite ends of the pool. Angie prepared herself with the stopwatch. From a distance she watched the way Angie spoke to Rachel, slightly bent to stay on the same level, gesturing with her other hand resting on Rachel's shoulder.

It was a privilege to see Angie in action, the warm efficiency with which she organized the team. Hannah looked forward to telling her that she was as good a coach as Hannah had always imagined she would be. She made a mental note to do that when this was all over.

As she anticipated the last length, Hannah's gaze flicked between whoever was in the water and Angie. Angie nodded reassuringly to each swimmer as they completed their lap.

At the conclusion of the run-through, the team clustered around their coach for feedback. There was something off. Though Hannah had no sense of what might be wrong, she could tell by the way Angie tapped at her teeth with a finger, eyeing the spreadsheet on her sheet of paper.

"That was excellent, thank you. Now we're going to try something different. I want Hannah to lead off, and Rachel you're going to be the anchor."

There was shuffling among the team; Andrea put a hand on her hip and Meghan grunted softly.

"What's up?" Angie said.

By unspoken agreement, the team members all looked toward Meghan. In her early twenties, Meghan had a reputation for dogged determination in the water and for speaking her mind.

"It's just that Rachel's the fastest. Why wouldn't she be race leader?"

"She's the fastest *sometimes*. When it comes to speed, Hannah and Rachel are more or less interchangeable, but Hannah tends to reverse the trend when it comes to training versus competition. Her times on race day are often better than during training. It's likely that she'll secure a greater lead going in. Okay?"

"Sure, we can try it," Meghan said grudgingly.

At the relay's end, they formed around Angie expectantly.

"How did we do?" Rachel said breezily. Of the four of them, she seemed to Hannah to be the most neutral party. Maybe she liked the idea of being the anchor.

"A teeny bit slower. Not enough to determine clearly. We'll give it more thought as we train, but at this stage, that's the way we're going with. That's how we're going to train from now on," Angie said.

"No disrespect to Rachel, but she's the least experienced. I don't know if she should anchor. What does Stuart think about all this? Does he know?" Meghan asked. "It might be completely different when there are swimmers in the lanes on either side of us."

Angie's green eyes flashed at Meghan for a moment before she smoothed her expression. "I'm taking that into consideration. And yes Meghan, Stuart's the head coach. It will be discussed with him, of course."

Throughout the remainder of the session, Andrea and Meghan murmured under their breath. Angie kept up her usual chipper manner, but it had to be getting under her skin. More than anything, Angie wanted to be taken seriously as a coach.

In the changing room, Hannah toweled off after her shower. Tonight was her own time, and she was looking forward to being alone. Rachel had rinsed off quickly, and now she sat nearby lacing up her white high-top sneakers. When Andrea and Meghan emerged from the showers, she caught the annoyance in Meghan's tone.

"I just hate the way the women's teams are treated. We get the consolation coach. I heard Jack and Stuart are both working with the men's team."

Andrea unwrapped a towel from her head, leaning over and scrunching her hair in it. "I know. She was a great swimmer, but I'm just not sure that Kelly Bundy out there is a great coach."

"Who's Kelly Bundy?" Rachel asked.

"You might be too young to know it," Hannah said. "But I think she's calling Angie stupid. It's pretty rude."

"Not being rude, I just wish we'd gotten a different coach, that's all," Andrea replied, shrugging. "You and Rachel will be fine, you'll get places in your individual races. This might be my only chance for a gold. There's a lot more riding on it for us."

Meghan pushed Andrea, but she was laughing. "Speak for yourself! I might take one, you never know."

Hannah pulled on her jeans. "Andrea, that has nothing to do with it. I want to do well in the relay just like you guys. I'm not in this only for myself."

"Why don't you guys like Angie? I think she's so nice. She's been super encouraging toward me," Rachel said.

"Nobody ever said she wasn't nice," Meghan snapped. "Rachel, we got the least experienced coach. Stuart is obviously the best, but Jack helped coach the team to Atlanta, and he knows what he's doing. They're using Angie to practice on us, can't you see that? And you should care more. You're supposed to be race leader. She gave Hannah your spot."

"Whoa!" Hannah said. "That's not cool, Meghan."

"Sorry. It's not personal against you, Hannah, you're a great swimmer. But you know Rachel should be first. And you've got more experience anyway. You should anchor. There's more than one reason why this is stupid."

Hannah leaned against the locker. She always gave coaches the benefit of the doubt; even that bully Tim had profited from her belief in a coach's authority.

This situation was unique, though. There were questions Hannah should ask herself. Were her feelings for Angie affecting her reactions? And more to the point, had Angie's decision making been impaired by what had been going on between them?

Meghan, Rachel, and Andrea stared back at her. Meghan's nostrils flared, and Rachel's face crumpled, a sheen over her eyes. Hannah chewed on her thumbnail. She had to do something.

"We shouldn't be arguing like this," she said. "Disagreements are okay, but they can't get heated."

After a moment, Meghan nodded. "You're right. I shouldn't have said that."

"So, what do we do? I don't think we can just leave it; this is too big an issue. Should we talk to Stuart?" Andrea asked.

"Behind her back? I don't think that's a good idea," Hannah said.

"Yeah, it'll just make us look like complainers," Meghan said. "Let's talk to Angie and see if we can get her to reconsider. We can go to her together. She seems like she'd be pretty reasonable. Don't you think?"

"I don't want to do that! She'll think we don't believe in her," Rachel said.

"We don't believe in her, though," Andrea pointed out, and Rachel directed a pleading look toward Hannah.

Hannah pushed herself off the locker. Nobody in this room knew it, but this was her mess, and it was her responsibility to put it right. "Okay. Do you guys trust me to talk to her myself? I just think it'll be less confrontational for her that way. But if she stands by her decision, especially after she's met with Stuart, we have to fall in line."

She looked around the room with her eyebrows raised, waiting until each person had signaled their agreement.

Angie was still in the aquatic center, sitting cross-legged on a bench seat, leaning back against the brick wall. On her lap were the statistics she'd been consulting, and she was using a gold pen to mark the margins. At the sound of Hannah's approaching footsteps, she looked up.

"Hey. Can I talk to you for a second?" Hannah asked.

"What's up?"

"Nothing. I just need to check something out with you. Why have you put me in the first position?"

Angie put the papers down on the bench at her side and raised herself from her seat until they stood eye to eye. "I explained my rationale clearly during the training session."

"I know," Hannah said, faltering. "I don't mean to question your judgment or anything."

"Except that you are. What's the problem here?"

"The team has some concerns."

Angie's chin was raised. "I know. Then why isn't the rest of the team coming to me? Why you?"

She glanced around to be sure they were alone. Then she stepped closer to Angie, mentally batting away all the things she noticed in an instant—the smell of Angie's hair, and her perfume. The way her eyes widened every time they were close like this.

"I thought it was best to talk to you alone. I just needed to know...You didn't put me in the first position for any other reason, did you?"

Calmly, Angie picked up the sheets of paper from the bench and handed them to Hannah. "A lot of time and energy has been put into picking through these numbers. You can go through them yourself if you like."

Hannah jogged her leg up and down, pushing the paper back toward Angie. "C'mon, no, I don't need to do that. I trust your judgment."

"You're not acting like it."

"I just needed to hear you say it, all right? I feel bad. I don't want to cause any problems. I just want to make sure that you're not doing this out of guilt."

Angie stared back at her. "Not everything is about that. We're never going to get past it, are we?"

She set her jaw. "Okay, sorry. Let's just focus on this then, can we?"

"You know that you and Rachel are close and the rest is a judgment call. My gut says that this order will work better. I'm a new coach, so of course they're going to question me. You don't have to indulge it. They look up to you. If you don't undermine me, maybe they won't."

"I wasn't undermining you," Hannah said, articulating each word carefully. She looked over her shoulder again. "I wouldn't do that to you. See, this is the reason why we should have held off from…being intimate. This conversation would be completely different if we hadn't slept together."

Angie searched her face. Hannah rubbed her mouth, as though she could take the words back. This conversation had spun out of control.

After staring at Hannah, her expression blank, Angie picked up a bag from under the seat. "I'll talk to Stuart. But I'd be doing that regardless of your complaints. The final decision is ours."

"Of course," Hannah said, sticking her hands in her pockets, her face hot.

She returned to the change rooms, where she was sure everyone would still be waiting for her to report back. She had no idea what she was going to tell them. And she had no idea what she was going to do about Angie.

CHAPTER TWENTY-FIVE

The disagreement with Angie had left a bad taste in Hannah's mouth, one she was impatient to wash out with some time alone and sleep.

The accommodation for the training period was dorm-like, the quarters uniform. Each room was bare, save for a bed, a nightstand, and a small desk. There were shared amenities, but she was grateful the rooms were single occupancy. Rachel stayed in the room adjoining hers. The night before, they'd spent the evening chatting in a common room, but she wasn't in a mood to socialize now.

In the bathroom, she brushed her teeth and pressed a cold washcloth to her face. The thing with Angie didn't have to be a disaster. Tomorrow, she would find a way to get Angie alone and work things out. The rift was like a tear in a piece of clothing; the longer it went on, the more damage would be done.

She dressed in her striped flannel pajama pants, comforted by their familiar softness, then pulled on a black tank top. On the way back to her room, she figured she should at least check in on Rachel and say goodnight. The friction in the team had disturbed Rachel today, and she wanted to reassure her. She'd like to tell Rachel she was proud of her too, for standing up for what she thought was right, especially against a group of older swimmers. The team should have listened to her more.

When she reached Rachel's door, it was ajar, and she pushed it until it creaked open further.

Rachel was splayed out on her mattress, the blankets thrown back. She checked her watch. Only eight o'clock. When she opened the door, Rachel didn't stir at all. It was strange that she should be sleeping so deeply at this hour.

Hannah crept to the edge of the bed. Rachel's lamp cast a soft light over her.

"Rachel, are you sick?"

Heavy breath fell from Rachel's open mouth, and she was snoring. It seemed slower than it should be, even for someone who was asleep. Hannah put a hand on Rachel's shoulder, and still, she didn't move.

Hannah shook her gently and then harder.

"Huh?" Rachel said groggily, but she didn't crack open an eye.

Hannah looked toward the lamp on the nightstand, wondering if she should turn it off. A sheet of pills lay next to a half-full glass of water. That must be what was making Rachel seem so out of it. Hannah searched for a packet to see what it was. There was nothing there.

Hannah stepped back out of the room. It wasn't right to leave Rachel like this without knowing exactly what was going on. Would Hannah look silly if she called one of the team medics to check on Rachel? It might draw attention or start nasty rumors.

Hannah paced the hall, deciding that she should call Angie. Angie cared a lot about Rachel's welfare, and Hannah could trust her to be discreet if Rachel had taken something she shouldn't have.

Because Angie lived in Brisbane, it was safe to assume that she was staying in her own home during training. Angie's card was tucked into Hannah's purse, and she took it to the pay phone in the hall. As she dialed, she tried to think of a backup plan if this didn't work. Mercifully, Angie answered after a few rings.

"Hey Angie, it's Hannah. I'm calling about Rachel. I think she's taken something, and I didn't know what else to do."

It was quiet as Angie took it in. "Shit. Is she okay?"

"I think so, but she's sleeping heavily so I'm not sure. I mean, I'd call a medic if I thought something was very wrong, but I just don't know. Sorry, I didn't know what else to do."

"No, it's okay, of course. I'm glad you called me. I'll come over there, and we'll decide what to do. You'll keep an eye on her until I get there?"

While she waited, Hannah continued to pace, sticking her head into Rachel's room now and then to eye the rise and fall of her chest. Finally, Angie tapped on the door to their quarters, rushing toward Rachel's room when Hannah pointed to it.

Angie leaned over Rachel, head cocked to listen to her breathing. She reached for the sheet of medication. "This is what she took?"

"Yeah. I have no idea what it is. Do you know?"

Angie held the foil packet under the lamp, examining the small white pills and then turning it over. "Shit. I know this. This is Restoxx."

Angie gestured toward Hannah's room, and they walked there together, silent until the door was closed behind them.

"Is it bad? Do we need to call a doctor?"

"No. There is only one pill missing from the sheet, so she'll sleep it off. It's normal for it to knock you out like that. But I'll need to talk to her tomorrow. That stuff isn't good for you."

"What is it, exactly? Restoxx?"

"You don't know it? A lot of swimmers were using it when I was in the game. I guess some things never change. It's a sleeping pill. Everyone was taking it on the long flights to get enough sleep, to train, and everything. I took it once myself, but never again. It makes you do weird stuff. Some people sleepwalk on it, and you wake up feeling awful."

"I wonder where she got it?"

"It's prescription. Perfectly legal, but if Rachel's having trouble sleeping, I'd like to talk to her about her stress levels."

Hannah sat on the bed. "I think talking to her is a great idea. It was obvious when you were coaching us today that she really looks up to you."

Angie stood close to the bed, hesitating until Hannah dipped her head to indicate she should join her and sit.

"She looks up to you too," Angie said.

"I guess. Hey," Hannah said.

Angie faced her, one leg pulled up underneath herself on the mattress. It was so easy for Hannah to get lost in those eyes, in the flecks of gray against green. "What is it?"

"You don't have to brace yourself, Angie. I wanted to ask if we were okay? After today, I mean."

"Oh," Angie said, smoothing down her shorts to cover more of her thigh. "Yes, of course."

"And, I wanted to apologize for making you feel undermined. I wish I'd handled things differently, but I got caught up in my own stuff. You're a great coach like I knew you would be. What did you think I was going to say just now?"

Angie stared back at her before her gaze dropped, making Hannah conscious of the fact that she wasn't wearing a bra under her tank top.

Angie averted her eyes. "I thought you were going to give me the speech."

"What speech is that?"

Her hand inched closer to Angie's knee. The distance between them today had been vast, their connection stretched to the breaking point. Hannah realized that her frustration hadn't been just with Andrea and Meghan. It was with herself, and with having to deny her attraction to Angie, even for a few hours.

When they'd initiated the break, it was with the assumption that it would be easy for them to compartmentalize. That was naïve.

"The one about regretting what we did and saying that it could never happen again. Isn't that what you were hinting at today?"

"You think that's how I feel?" She slid her fingers onto Angie's bare knee, grasping smooth skin. In here, when they were alone, she didn't have to try to reject this feeling. "When I can't seem to keep my hands off you?"

"You do apparently have an issue with resisting me right now. Is it my slippers?" Angie said, a smile tugging at her lips. She waved her foot in the air. "They turn you on?"

"That must be it."

Flattening her palm, Hannah brushed it over Angie's knee, moving it upward. Quiet fell over the room as Hannah ran her hand over Angie's legs.

They shifted closer, Angie curling a hand around the back of Hannah's neck. They were near enough that Angie's breath touched Hannah's lips. But for another heart-stopping minute, Hannah only rubbed Angie, fingers playing over her inner thighs.

At last, they closed the distance, making out while Hannah explored the silky skin under her fingers. A moment later Angie shoved her hand under Hannah's tank top, reaching upward quickly. When she grabbed Hannah's breast, Hannah arched into her.

"Shhh," Angie said, giggling into her mouth. "We have to be quiet."

They kissed while Angie teased the undersides of her breasts, and Hannah bit back a moan. After a few minutes, Angie drew back.

"You're not that good at not making noise!" Angie whispered hoarsely.

Hannah grinned back at her. "We'll see how good you are at staying quiet."

Hannah stood and pushed Angie back onto the mattress. She dragged Angie by the legs to pull her further down the bed. Hannah yanked Angie's shorts and underwear down her legs to the sound of Angie's quickened breath. Angie kicked them onto the ground.

By the single bed, Hannah kneeled. When she paused to look up, Angie was lying with the back of her hand over her mouth, biting a knuckle, trying her best to be silent.

Afterward, they lay in one another's arms on the narrow bed, Angie stroking Hannah's hair.

"I should go," Angie said.

She tightened her arms around Angie's waist. "Stay with me, just for a little while?"

"Okay."

Angie rolled onto her side, propping herself up on an elbow to look down into Hannah's face. She dropped a kiss onto her forehead, then she just watched her, tracing a finger over Hannah's collarbone.

"What are you thinking about?" Hannah asked.

"We're not doing too well at this, are we? Taking a break, I mean?"

"I guess not. Does that bother you?"

"Yes. I'm so scared of history repeating itself. Aren't you?"

"Please stop worrying. I know how to focus when I'm in the pool. It hasn't compromised my training at all. I know things got weird today, but there's no way of knowing...with all our history...it might have happened like that either way. We'll never know."

"I guess you're right..."

"Besides, if you want to know the truth, it would be more distracting for me if we didn't do this."

"How do you mean? Why would you be distracted?"

Hannah put her hand on Angie's cheek, stroking it with her thumb. "Because you're all I can think about right now anyway."

Angie kissed her, then snuggled into her. The moment was so perfect that Hannah wanted it to last forever. She bit back her questions about whether there was any future for them after the Games. Was this a fling or something more? The issues had been hanging in the air between them, but in these stolen moments how could they talk about anything serious?

Instead of talking, she contemplated what Marie said about not really knowing Angie. It had sounded true when Marie said it, but at times like these, she saw the foolishness of questioning the link between herself and Angie. She had seen enough to know who Angie was. Some things couldn't be described and didn't make sense on the face of it.

She knew how it felt when Angie pressed herself against her like she was right now, as though she never wanted to let go. Hannah allowed her eyes to drop shut, floating in Angie's arms.

CHAPTER TWENTY-SIX

2000 - Sydney Olympic Games

Finally, it was happening, as near to perfect as anything Hannah had ever experienced. With the benefit of adult confidence and a mature understanding of what it meant to be at the Games, Hannah was on cloud nine.

She had taken it for granted that she had a solid grasp of what to expect from this event. That was wrong; the combination of the Games being hosted in her home country and the fact that it was the millennium year brought a different energy. When Hannah became part of the audience to support fellow Australians, she giggled at the chant that the Aussies had taken up: "Aussie, Aussie, Aussie." It was thrilling to think they'd be yelling it for her, soon enough.

The swimming finals began only a few days after the opening ceremony, and the relay event was Hannah's first competition. Before the race, the four members of the team clasped hands with their heads bowed, cementing their commitment to one another. The day after their argument about positions, Hannah called a team meeting to hash things out. They eventually agreed they would cast any reservations aside and put their faith in Angie.

By now, they believed in the order. Their times during training were impressive. If the plan was controversial, so much the better. Surprising people was fun.

Angie strode into the locker room. It took knowing her well to see how edgy she was, to look for the clenched jaw and a light tremble in her fingers.

Angie asked, "How are we all feeling?"

"Ready to squash those Americans like a bug. No offense," Meghan said.

Angie held up her hands. "Hey, none taken. I'd love to see that. You ladies have been a pleasure to coach. I have absolute faith in all of you."

The circle widened to include her, and they stood with their arms around one another while she spoke quietly to them about determination and focus, about not allowing themselves to get distracted. They broke, Angie's and Hannah's eyes meeting across the circle.

"All right, let's get out there," Andrea said, punching a fist into her other palm.

"I'll be with you in a sec, I want to use the bathroom one last time," Hannah said.

Angie picked up on Hannah's signal and stayed behind. The sounds of other women showering and talking came from the next room, but there was nobody else around. Hannah hugged Angie to draw strength from her.

In the last weeks, there had been many more meetings. They'd risked getting caught, with Angie sneaking into her room during training and at the village as often as she could. Now and then one of them would suggest they dial it back, but they could never follow through. They touched but never talked, at least not about what they were doing.

"Are you okay?" Angie asked.

"You mean aside from feeling like I'm going to throw up?"

They swayed together, and Hannah pressed her lips to Angie's jawline.

"No matter what happens, I'm proud of you. As a coach and as a friend," Angie said, fumbling the last word.

"I'm proud of you too. You've done an amazing job with us. Rachel's confidence has gone through the roof over this last little while. I think it's going to make all the difference."

"Thank you. Good luck."

"You're my good luck charm," Hannah said as she gripped Angie's shoulders.

"You have to go," Angie said, twirling her around and pushing her. "Get out there."

"Bye!" she said, as though they were parting after dinner or she was leaving for work.

"Bye, love you!" Angie said, through a giggle.

Hannah's step slowed, and she looked back over her shoulder. Angie's smile had frozen.

"Hannah!" Meghan said from the door. "You've got to hurry up!"

"Coming, coming!" Hannah replied, beckoning for Angie to follow.

They were at the Olympic Games, and even now she was more worried about Angie than anything else. Time to shake it off and put on her game face. They were going to win this.

When Hannah had touched the wall, there was time to check how she'd done. In the water, it felt like her lead was excellent; she'd defeated the swimmers in the lanes on either side of her. It was even better than she'd calculated.

Until this instant, there was a part of her that had never quite believed in Angie's strategy. From the beginning she'd gotten behind Angie's idea, knowing that she had to back her one hundred percent and doing her best to shove any negativity away.

Hannah had been right to disregard it. While she watched Rachel powering down the lane like some kind of aquatic cheetah, Hannah cheered her on. Rachel was neck and neck with the American swimmer on her left.

When a race was this close, it was impossible to tell who was going to take it, but she had a good feeling. There was no time to seek out Angie, and she wished she were standing right here with her so they could watch it together.

At the end, there was an agonizing uncertain second, before that deafening chant rang out. Aussie Aussie Aussie.

The four of them ran to each other, hugging and jumping up and down, then they folded Angie into the group. Hannah couldn't stop beaming. The weight of Angie's arm was on her shoulder, and in the chaos of the win, she snuck a kiss on Angie's cheek.

They stole more than a kiss when Angie came to Hannah's room later. As Hannah pulled Angie's shirt over her head, astride her on the single mattress, Angie put a hand on Hannah's chest.

"Wait...what about tomorrow! I shouldn't be here. I came to say congratulations, but I was going to let you rest," Angie said, running her hand down Hannah's torso. "You kind of put all your eggs in one basket with the two hundred. Surely we can wait one night?"

"You scared you're going to wear me out?" Hannah said, twisting against Angie, hips pressing into her waist.

"That sounds like a challenge to me," Angie said, pulling Hannah downward.

The next morning Hannah scrubbed a hand over her face. She surveyed her body and scanned her mind. This would likely be the only time she'd have alone before the madness started, and she wanted to soak it up.

Angie was right. She hadn't slept as much as she should have. It wasn't important. Every extra moment spent with Angie was worth it. There was no logic to it, but she was sure it gave her vitality. This morning there was a force flowing through her; all her strength and mental energy were invested in the competition.

Angie was right about this too; she had gambled by focusing only on the two-hundred-meter event. The decision to return had been made late in the game, and she had worried about spreading herself too thin. It meant that she only had one shot, and she wasn't going to waste it.

On the block, she focused on the solid tile beneath her bare feet. How many times had she stood just like this, primed to dive in? Hundreds, probably thousands of times.

It was so strange to think that this might be the last one of any significance. It was an ending; she was closing a loop in her life.

She had to win, for herself and for Angie. It would always be strange between them if she didn't. Taking the gold was the only way to right a wrong. This time she'd live up to her potential.

The crowd raised their voices for Hannah and Rachel too, who was a couple of lanes away. "Aussie, Aussie, Aussie." Hannah wanted to make them cheer louder, to bring the house down.

One of the many advantages of Sydney hosting the games was the fact that everyone Hannah loved could be here. Her parents, Mark and Ethan and their partners, Marie and Scott, and Debbie.

And of course, there was Angie. There was no point denying that Angie belonged in the group of people that she loved. With searing clarity given to her by the weight of this day, she understood how far she'd fallen. It had gone beyond infatuation long ago; she loved Angie more than she'd ever loved anyone before.

She loved the way Angie smelled and the touch of her skin, adored the sound of her voice and every expression that passed across her face.

Priming herself to dive in, she recognized she had to tell Angie how she felt, and soon. How could she have so much courage when it came to swimming, and so little about making a confession about these feelings to her? There was no future without her in it.

But right now, she was going to swim.

Surging through the pool, she sensed the American favorite, Jodie Bell, was close in the lane next to her. It couldn't be a distraction, only a fact. She stroked cleanly through the water. Working, always working, to do the best she could.

The mantra spooled out in her mind. She had to win. What was she here for, if not to win? She had to want it more than everyone else.

At the turn, she was euphoric. She was pushing herself, increasing her speed as much as she could.

Coming up to the finish, she gave it an extra push. The race was close all the way, and all she knew for sure was that she and Jodie were neck and neck. Pushing under the lane dividers, Hannah and Rachel came together, clutching one another while the announcer made the call.

Hannah first, Jodie second. Rachel had the bronze medal.

Rachel cried, her tears mingling with the water already on her face. Hannah held her, rubbing her back in the water.

"We did it, girl. I'm proud of you," Hannah said.

Hannah shook hands with Jodie, and they slapped one another on the back firmly in congratulations. At times like these, it always seemed stupid to Hannah for them to be on opposing teams. They were all swimmers, in this together.

Proudly, the three of them stood side-by-side on the dais. Holding Rachel's hands, Hannah and Jodie reassured her not to worry. Though it might feel like her legs were going to give out, she was going to be okay.

Hannah smiled broadly when the medal was placed around her neck. Not bad, for someone her age. Two for two was not bad at all, considering how long she'd been retired. Finally, she could call herself an Olympic gold medalist. She'd helped add two medals to the count, and now her work was done.

Though she'd just been lamenting the existence of teams, the Australian anthem brought a lump to her throat.

The press conference followed, and Hannah was left with a couple of hours before she was due at dinner. Her folks had booked a table in a swanky Sydney restaurant for everyone who'd traveled up from Melbourne.

Stuart had been the representative from the coaching team at the press conference, and so Hannah hadn't even laid eyes on Angie since she'd gotten out of the water. Her priority was to get to her room for a nap, but the first thing she planned to do when she got up was to find her.

Hannah was walking toward the shuttle bus that would take her back to the village when there was a tap on her shoulder.

"Angie!" she said, and they joined in an embrace.

There were too many people surrounding them for more than that, but they made the most of it, Angie's hands splayed across Hannah's back. "Congratulations," Angie whispered into her hair. "I always knew you could do it."

"Thank you for believing in me."

They faced one another, and Hannah wished the rest of the world would fall away. She'd never wanted to kiss anyone so much in her life. Angie was staring at her lips too.

"Will you come to my dinner tonight?" she said. They were still holding hands, and Hannah realized she didn't care who saw it.

"I wish I could, but we've got an official event. Come to my place after?" Angie said.

"You can count on it."

As she strolled away, she looked back over her shoulder. Angie was watching her go.

Hannah wanted so badly to stop leaving her. If she had her way, she'd never walk away from her again.

CHAPTER TWENTY-SEVEN

Hannah rapped faintly on Angie's hotel room door. When Angie opened it, she appeared in a bright red silk robe, her hair fashioned into a messy bun.

The instant Hannah was inside she molded her hands over Angie's waist. She was walking Angie back toward the bed, tongue flicking devilishly into her sweet mouth when something caught her eye.

On the nightstand, there was a stuffed toy, a mermaid with a purple clam-shell bra and bright pink hair.

"What's that?"

"Oh, that?" Angie replied with flushed cheeks. "I wanted to get you something. I just thought it would be funny for you to have something to take back with you to Melbourne. You can cuddle it and think of me, or whatever."

Hannah picked it up, biting her lip and smiling. She moved the arm on the mermaid, making her wave. "This is so cute."

"I know it's a little silly. But mermaids always make me think of you."

"She's not silly, I love her," Hannah said, propping the toy against the lamp.

Hannah perched on the mattress, patting it until Angie sat next to her. Angie put an arm around Hannah's shoulders. "Big day. Biggest day, really. You did it. I'm so happy and proud of you."

"It'll sink in that it's over in about a week."

"How are you feeling about…"

"Go on," Hannah said softly.

Was Angie going to ask her about their future, at last? On the one hand, Hannah was sure Angie felt the same way as she did. Her emotions were parceled up in every touch and kiss, and her eyes held the same tenderness that was in Hannah. But on the other, Angie had made no move toward talking to her about anything. They both knew she had plans to go back to America, and that was that.

They were still behaving like the awkward teenagers they'd been when they first met. Both too shy somehow to make the first move and talk. Focusing on their physical connection was easy, but Hannah wondered, since when did having lots of sex make you an adult? The world had it backward. The sex was the easy part.

What were they so afraid of?

Finally, Angie started. "I just wanted to make sure you're okay. I know you got everything you could have dreamed of. You couldn't have done better. But I remember there can sometimes be that big mood crash when it's all over. You're retired now. So it really is all over, and there's nothing else to get ready for."

Angie was looking at her with a furrowed brow, and it made her smile.

"Did I say the wrong thing, or something?"

"Of course not. Just not what I thought you were going to say, that's all."

Angie circled Hannah's wrist with her fingers. "I'm tired, aren't you? I haven't been sleeping so well. Can you please lie down with me?"

"Sure. I want to talk about some stuff, anyway." Angie shot her a wary look that was hard to decipher.

"Wait, I want to put on some music. I brought my CD player," Angie said, bustling over to the portable radio set up on the gray carpet, near the wall. "Will you think I'm cheesy if I play '80s stuff?"

"Not at all, I'd love that," Hannah replied. Maybe Angie was just too tired to talk about anything important. But if they didn't speak now, when would they? Time was running out.

Slipping off her shoes, Hannah watched Angie loosen the belt of her robe. Underneath it, her shorts were brief enough to reveal her lovely thighs. With them, she wore a cream-colored sleeveless top with spaghetti straps. A song by The Cure played low; the melancholy sound opening a well of nostalgia.

Hannah reclined on the hard mattress, and when Angie joined her, she gathered her up in her arms. They spooned, Hannah brushing Angie's shoulder and then lowering her mouth to it.

"Do you mind if we just lie here for a while?" Angie asked.

"Whatever you want, baby," Hannah said, the pet name tasting sweet in her mouth. She'd always thought talk like that was lame, but everything was different with Angie.

"We can have sex if you want…"

Hannah rubbed Angie's shoulder. "I thought you were tired. You just said you wanted to lie here."

Angie's shoulder moved under her hand as she shrugged. "I'm just saying we could if you wanted to, that's all."

"Wait, so let me get this straight. You're offering to have sex with me even though you just said you're too tired to do anything but lie here. Why?"

Another shrug. It wasn't like Angie to expect Hannah to read her mind, and it was growing more concerning by the minute that she wouldn't say anything. Hannah's mind raced.

"Okay, Angie. I would hope that you'd know me well enough by now to understand that I would never, ever want to have sex with you if you didn't want to. You've never done that before, have you?"

"No," Angie said sharply. "I haven't."

Hannah's hand dropped from Angie's shoulder. "Well, then why would you say that to me? Do you think sex is all that I want from you? That I'd use you like that?"

"Don't."

"I don't know what else to think!" Hannah said, hating how she sounded.

This was not at all what she'd expected from tonight. She'd won. If there needed to be an evening of the scales, it had happened and they could meet one another as equals now. So, why weren't things better between them? Hannah wished they could rewind and start over again. The Cure song had flipped into the next, more depressing than the last.

"Well, that makes two of us!"

Hannah propped herself on her elbow. "Okay, please, can you turn and face me? Can you at least do that?"

Slowly, Angie rolled onto her back, staring up at the ceiling. Hannah took Angie's chin between her fingers, gently tilting her face toward her.

"What did you mean by that? You don't know what to think about what, exactly?"

Angie lifted her hands and dropped them helplessly back onto her stomach. "How am I supposed to know what you think or what you want? You've never told me much about either of those things. Not these days, anyway."

Hannah's mouth fell open. "What? You haven't told me either! That seems a little unfair! Until now I thought we were on the same page? That we were seeing how things went."

"Yeah, we were but…Then we've been together so many times, and I have no idea how you feel about me."

Hannah's temper had been boiling, but now she began to soften. "That's what I wanted to talk to you about. It's past time we talked about things. I couldn't agree more with that."

Angie had been staring at the ceiling again, but now her gaze snapped back to Hannah's eyes.

Hannah could see that Angie was afraid. So was she, but this was too important to not speak from her heart. Part of Hannah hated that they were in the middle of an argument when she was going to say this, but she couldn't wait one more minute. If she'd known how much the uncertainty was affecting Angie, she would have done this so much sooner.

Maybe the strength of her emotions toward Angie meant that she was far ahead of her, but she couldn't worry about that. She would wait for as long as it took for Angie to catch up to her.

"Where are you going?"

"Don't worry, don't worry. I'm not going anywhere. I just want to do this right," Hannah said, climbing down from the bed. She knelt on the carpet, before Angie. She leaned forward, putting her elbows on Angie's knees.

"What are you doing..."

"Let me get this out," she said. She clasped Angie's hands and looked into her eyes. "You say you don't know how I feel about you, so let me tell you. From the moment we saw one another again, I began to understand that it was never going to be over between us. That I never wanted it to be."

Angie stared back at her, tightening her grip on Hannah's hands.

Hannah wet her lips and went on. "We talked about having a pause. As far as I'm concerned, we were on a pause for ten long years. I don't need any more time. That's the last thing I want. If you'll have me, I want to be with you. I love you."

Angie laughed through tears, clutching Hannah's face now, pressing her hair into the sides of her head. "I love you too."

"Really?"

"Of course, I do! Couldn't you see I've been chasing you since I saw you again? I was worried I was embarrassing myself sometimes. I've been a woman on a mission."

"Well, mission accomplished," Hannah said. The kiss they shared was so tender it made her ache. "God, I'm so relieved. To be completely honest with you, I was worried. I thought maybe this was some whirlwind holiday romance. Not a holiday, but you know what I mean. I didn't know whether to believe that it was real."

"Real as the nose on your face," Angie said, putting a finger on the tip of Hannah's nose.

"I don't think that's exactly right, but I'm happy to go with it," Hannah said.

They kissed again, Angie wrapping her arms around Hannah's neck. "So, what happens now? We do the long-distance thing for a while?"

"Why? Do you really want to go back to America?" The smile could split her face. Why had they waited so long for this?

"Not long-term. But that was the plan. You know that!"

"Then let's not do things half-assed. You've never sounded that excited about going back there, and you can get a job here instead. Move in with me."

Laughter bubbled from Angie, and she covered her mouth.

"Hey. Don't laugh!"

"It's nervous laughter. Do you mean that?"

Hannah sat back on her heels. If Angie said yes, she'd be able to look at that face as much as she wanted. Every day and forever. Angie had never been more beautiful.

"Well, what do you think? It doesn't have to be for always. We can go over to America sometime, move back and forth like you wanted when we were younger. I just feel like it makes sense to do it this way for a while when I have the house and everything."

"Everyone's going to think we're crazy!" Angie said, a hand over her mouth.

"Let them say it. I don't want to be apart."

They threw their arms around one another. Hannah pulled something from her pocket, draping it around Angie's neck. Angie looked down at the heavy medallion and cackled.

"Your medal? Really?"

"We earned it together. Gold looks good on you."

Hannah climbed back onto the bed, sinking into Angie's embrace.

CHAPTER TWENTY-EIGHT

With an arm hooked around Hannah's waist, Angie sighed. Hannah burrowed in against her so that their temples touched.

"It's so nice to have everything unpacked. I feel so grown up and settled."

"Aw! You finally have a home!" Hannah said, lightly shaking Angie by the shoulder.

"Why don't you quit joking around and hang that picture of mine? You're taller than me," Angie said, pushing Hannah toward the wall.

"You've got it, short stack," Hannah said.

Hannah used the hammer she'd borrowed from Mark to drive in the golden nail, then positioned the print. The framed photograph was of the ocean, and from this close, all Hannah could see was the white lip of a glittering wave.

"How does it look from back there? Do you think it's even?"

"Up on the left a little...not that far. Down. It's still a bit crooked, can you pull it down on the right?"

Hannah's arms dropped, and she twisted around. "Are you just messing with me now? Having a little fun at my expense?"

Angie clapped her hands together, laughing. "It's perfect now. I just wanted to watch you. Nice buns."

Hannah shook her head and went to Angie for a hug. Hanging the picture was the last piece of work to make the townhouse *theirs* as opposed to *hers*.

In the weeks before Angie arrived, Hannah had worked to clear out her old solitary life, the one that didn't have Angie in it. She'd sorted through every room and culled anything she didn't need. She couldn't believe how much junk she'd accumulated since moving in.

Now there was an empty drawer and a spare shelf in the bathroom. There was blank space in the cupboard in which Angie could hang her clothes. Hannah wanted everything to be perfect for her.

It kept Hannah occupied when she was wracked with anxiety about whether what they were doing was indeed crazy. It was so fast. Everyone kept telling her just how fast it was, even Viv. Their circumstances were dictating them moving in together, and maybe she shouldn't have suggested it.

Then Angie was here, bringing her warmth and her smile. As soon as she stepped through the gate at the airport, Hannah wondered what she had ever worried about.

It was the very best decision they could have ever made.

They kissed at a deliciously slow pace, Hannah beginning to form a hazy thought that they should take it upstairs. They'd already christened every room in the townhouse, and the floor down here was hard and unforgiving.

She sprang from Angie when the front door opened, and she put a hand on her chest, panting. "Jesus, Marie! It's not just me here anymore."

"Sorry!" Marie said, pointing her finger back and forth between them. "But it looks like I got here just in time. I love you both, but I do not want to see that."

"Well that's easily fixed. Learn to knock like a normal person!" Hannah said.

"And ruin my irresistible charm? I'm spontaneous! It's part of my schtick. I don't think so."

Marie hugged each of them and kissed them on the cheek. During the short time Angie had been in Melbourne, she'd endeared herself to Hannah's best friend with impressive ease. When Hannah first told Marie about Angie moving in so quickly, Marie was ruthless in telling her they were making a big mistake and that they should put the brakes on.

Marie's predictions quickly turned around when Angie charmed her and Scott, insisting on cooking and baking for them. The way to Marie's heart was through her stomach, and it gave Angie plenty of time to do what she was good at. They talked until Marie warmed up, after being sent home with plates of leftovers.

All that food served another purpose; it convinced Marie that Angie knew her stuff.

Marie opened her bag and unpacked the contents. A heavy laptop, notebooks, and a giant folded map of Melbourne covered the table.

"What's this evening's project?" Angie asked, tying her hair back and pushing up her sleeves.

"Tonight, we're going to talk about location. There are a few spaces I want to discuss with you, then we can narrow down further before we go to look at them."

"Fantastic!" Angie said, smoothing her hands over the map.

"Don't get too excited. It gets pretty boring until we get to actually go and look, and at least some of them are going to be dumps. I think I've got a lead on a couple of good spots, though. Oh, did you guys check out that new list of chefs I sent you?"

Hannah nodded. "We did. There are a couple more that we'd love to test out."

"Good. All those people come highly recommended. Do you still think you want to try and get a female chef?"

"Yeah, I think so," Angie said. It was a male-dominated industry, and she liked the idea of giving a woman the opportunity.

One of Hannah's favorite things about this venture was the hunt for a chef to poach, which meant a lot of food testing. It was a great excuse to have long dinners where they sampled as many items as they could from a menu. Because Angie loved food but wasn't a professional, they needed someone creative but dependable to run the kitchen.

"Well that's good," Marie said. "Statistically more women are vegetarian too, right? So, you'll have a better chance of getting a good one."

"They don't have to actually be vegetarian, though, just good at veggie cooking. And versatile. We want someone who can do an extensive range so that even meat eaters will want to go there," Hannah said.

"Sure, but it'd help, I think. Hey, maybe you'll get another lezzie too," Marie said.

"Marie! You don't get to say that word."

"Sorry. You know what I meant. Okay, now, I've narrowed down the location hunt for somewhere that's inner city where the hipsters will hang out. The rent on a building will be more expensive, but it'll be worth it. You need somewhere central because like I've told you before, a vegetarian restaurant is just not going to work out in the burbs."

"I'm going to leave this part to you guys. I still don't know Melbourne very well," Angie said.

Hannah watched while Marie traced around the map with a finger. She jotted down a list in the notebook they were calling the "restaurant bible."

Before they progressed to the next step, Marie refolded the map and capped her pen. "I need to talk to you both about something."

"What's the problem? Are you going to tell us we don't have enough money or something?" Hannah said, arms crossed.

"No, nothing like that. I just…There's something I've wanted to talk to you about since you asked me to help. I may have chickened out once or twice."

Angie was rinsing a glass in the sink, and when Marie beckoned her over with a hand, she put it in the drainer and sat back down at the table. Sensing they might not like what they were about to hear, Hannah grabbed Angie's hand under the table.

"Okay. Let us have it," Hannah said.

Though she felt like warning Marie to be very careful about what she might be about to say, she was helping them almost free of charge. They owed her the courtesy of listening.

Marie slowly pushed out a breath. "Here goes. The restaurant business is a very stressful one. A lot of restaurants fail after the first year or so."

"Oh, is that what this is about?" Hannah asked. "You may be forgetting that you've given us this speech already! We've taken steps to protect ourselves financially, and we're not sinking everything into this."

"Shh!" Marie said, holding up a finger. "That's not where I was going. I'm not worried about your money. I'm worried about your relationship."

Angie held Hannah's hand more tightly under the table. "Why?"

"Normally I'd be having this conversation a little sooner in the piece, as it's part of my job. But it's harder to say this stuff to friends. I don't just say it to couples. I tell anyone who's planning on going in to business together. That includes families. But it goes double for couples, and especially for you two, given that this is a new relationship. You're living together, and now you're going to be working together. Are you sure you're up for all of this?"

Marie's shoulders were drawn up tightly. Angie bowed her head toward Hannah, indicating that she should take this one. Hannah reached across the table and put a hand on Marie's arm.

"Thank you, Marie. I appreciate you looking out for us. But we've talked about that, and we're confident we can work through it. We didn't just talk about protecting ourselves financially. We're taking on different parts of the business so that we won't be living in one another's pockets, and we'll be checking in with one another every step of the way. We both really want to do this."

There was a long silence while they all looked at one another, and finally, Marie let out an exaggerated sigh of relief. "Oh my god, I was so scared to say that to you, but you've really thought of everything, haven't you?"

Angie's hand was on Hannah's knee now.

"You know what? I think we have."

Marie leaned back in her chair. "You know I was skeptical about all of this. Angie, I'm sure Hannah's told you. But I'm happy to say when I'm wrong. You two...I think you two are the real deal. You're in this for the long haul, I think."

Hannah shrugged. There was no need to say it when she was sure that time would bear it out. People would see for themselves.

Hannah and Angie were drowning in one another, but they had their eyes open. They could always see the shore.

They were in those deep waters together now, and Hannah couldn't think of a better way to be.

Bella Books, Inc.

Women. Books. Even Better Together.

P.O. Box 10543
Tallahassee, FL 32302

Phone: 800-729-4992
www.bellabooks.com

CPSIA information can be obtained
at www.ICGtesting.com
Printed in the USA
JSHW032006160320
4775JS00001BA/3